WHISPER
ALLEY

WHISPER
ALLEY

GREGORY MARCEL

CITI OF BOOKS

Copyright © 2024 by Gregory Marcel.

All rights reserved. No part of this publication may be reproduced, distributed, or transmitted in any form or by any means, including photocopying, recording, or other electronic or mechanical methods, without the prior written permission of the copyright owner and the publisher, except in the case of brief quotations embodied in critical reviews and certain other noncommercial uses permitted by copyright law. For permission requests, write to the publisher, addressed "Attention: Permissions Coordinator," at the address below.

CITIOFBOOKS, INC.
3736 Eubank NE Suite A1
Albuquerque, NM 87111-3579
www.citiofbooks.com
Hotline: 1 (877) 389-2759
Fax: 1 (505) 930-7244

Ordering Information:
Quantity sales. Special discounts are available on quantity purchases by corporations, associations, and others. For details, contact the publisher at the address above.

Printed in the United States of America.

ISBN-13:	Softcover	979-8-89391-331-6
	eBook	979-8-89391-332-3

Library of Congress Control Number: 2024919363

TABLE OF CONTENTS

CHAPTER ONE: The Rock 1

CHAPTER TWO: Cameko 12

CHAPTER THREE: Jonah's Tear...24

CHAPTER FOUR: The Ride..36

CHAPTER FIVE: Surprise..49

CHAPTER SIX: Field Day..59

CHAPTER SEVEN: Yuriko..69

CHAPTER EIGHT: Saturday..78

CHAPTER NINE: Hard Core...88

CHAPTER TEN: Run Cameko..100

CHAPTER ELEVEN: Love Hurts 110

CHAPTER TWELVE: Checking Out 124

CHAPTER THIRTEEN: Mr. Stewart...137

CHAPTER FOURTEEN: Fuji...148

CHAPTER FIFTEEN: The Gift..161

CHAPTER SIXTEEN: My Way 173

CHAPTER ONE
THE ROCK

The booming, commanding voice, yelling, "reveille, get out of the rack" awakened me! Fighting back the drug like trance that held me down for the last 6 hours, I gingerly sat up on my rack. We were in reception at Camp Foster. The Flying Tiger had arrived on Okinawa at 1:00 a. m. Asia time. The sleep turned out to be a blessing. We had stopped over at the U.S. Air Force Base over in South Korea. Some Marines were transported there for assignment. We had waited 12 hours at the base there not knowing when we'd fly again. By this time my Alpha uniform wasn't so crisp. I was self-conscience the rest of the flight.

As I stared at my surroundings, I realized I wasn't in a nightmare it was real. The open squad bay was a vivid reminder that I still served as a U.S. Marine. Sure, I loved it, and I wanted the accolades that went along with it. I had several phone numbers from women who otherwise would have nothing to do with me. I cleared the fog and got prepared to hit the showers. I quickly showered and dug into my duffel bag for my camouflage utilities. I found a plug next to the metal heater, which wasn't on, and I did my best to iron my field uniform.

As I went outside, the humid air hit me. I took shorter breaths to compensate, yet, still, the suffocating effects of the Okinawa morning rippled through my flesh. "Fall in!" the reception Sergeant expertly yelled, I quickly ran into the formation, "A-ten-huh! Listen Marines, after chow, you will report back to the reception center and then transportation will be provided to your duty station. Any questions?" The Sergeant a menacing yet skilled looking veteran then dismissed us for breakfast.

I hadn't really got to know anyone yet, so I walked with the pack over to the main chow hall. Fortunately, the chow hall was close by the barracks and we didn't have to march in formation. Typically, there was a long line snaking well outside of the chow hall. In my 8 months of being in the Marine Corps, I never ate at a chow hall that I didn't like. It must have been the adjustment of boot camp living that transformed my taste buds. My very first time eating in basic training, I relished it. After months of being marched around, drilling and being berated, I was so hungry at chow time that I became light headed. I observed that waiting in line was the one thing I'd have to get accustomed too.

The line steadily moved ahead and finally I signed in to the non-rate side of the line and stepped in the chow hall. Not bad, a large facility. I had to admit that even though Okinawa is an Island, everything was built with size in view. I zoned out as I went through the chow line. I wanted eggs, bacon, and toast. I motioned with my head on each item I wanted as I sidestepped through the line. It appeared that all the new-bee's, the people fresh on the Island, a military jargon, sat on one side and so did I.

I ate quickly without socializing. I was sure I'd meet scores of people, but for now I needed my instincts to guide me. I knew that coupled with training the military instincts would lead me to safely and successfully following orders. I put away my tray and headed out of the chow hall. It took less than 10 minutes to get back to the reception center. I knew what duty station I was headed too, Camp Kinser, but where that happened to be I had no clue. All I could do is accept it. I saw other Marines in the reception center who were waiting on their orders sitting around on their racks, so I did the same. In the meantime I tried to stay focused.

Two hours later we were all aboard military transportation called a cattle car. It was a tractor pulling a trailer that resembled a cattle carrier. Nonetheless, we settled in, begin the destination to the new bases. As we traveled, I looked out of the open-air cubicle window of the trailer. The Okinawa life was the exact opposite of America. People drove in the wrong direction. This could take some time getting used to. I watched in amazement how the Okinawan's were so uniform. The women, most of whom were petite, surprised me. I was sure that they were primitive women who only came out to take a break from their daily chores. But, no, these women were clean cut, sharply dressed females; I wanted one. As we turned the corner, my erection eased somewhat. A young man, I still carried a charge. And these miniature beauties had ignited a fire deep down inside of me. Even though I knew my obligation here in Okinawa to be one year, I felt that I'd at least say hi to one. The cattle truck stopped, the driver got out of the vehicle and yelled, "camp Kinser!" That was it; I gathered my belongings and eagerly stepped out of the vehicle. I strode toward Headquarters to turn in my records and get directions to my duty station.

Headquarters personnel quickly pointed out H&S Motor Pool. A very short walk, I gathered my belongings and headed to work. When I arrived, I braced myself. The Marines in this unit had murderous expressions on their faces. I shook with nervousness as the Sergeant ordered me to fall in as I arrived at morning formation. After formation, the officer in charge, wanted to talk with me. I excused myself from formation and reported as ordered. "Relax, lance corporal Walters, have a seat!" I gingerly sat down and faced the Second Lieutenant, called boot Louie by seasoned veterans. I dare not entertain the thought. The Lieutenant spoke first, "I'm Lieutenant Albert Wikenburg, and I run this motor pool Son!" The Lieutenant spoke rather forcefully. "Yes, Sir!" I didn't want to get on his bad side too quickly. "At ease Son! I know you're not accustomed to this Island lifestyle yet, but we do have Marines here who think they're running this operation." The officer looked questionably at me. I remained silent. "Well, Son, you follow orders and you'll be fine, that clear Marine!"

"Yes, Sir!" I gave the O.I.C. my undivided attention. He quickly stood; I did the same. "Sergeant Larson!" A stout looking combat ready Marine soon appeared at the office door, "Yes Sir!"

"Take lance corporal Walters down to the barracks and get him checked in."

"Come on Son, let's go!" I grabbed my bags and exclaimed, "yes, sir!" the Sergeant quickly corrected me, "I'm a Sergeant not an officer Marine!"

"Yes, Sergeant." I could hear the Lieutenant chuckle as I grabbed my belongings and followed the Sergeant. I observed the motor pool as I departed the office. It wasn't much, very small considering its relevance to the function of the company. It was neat though, extremely orderly and I had been informed stateside that things were tight on the rock. We rode in silence as the Sergeant personally drove me to the barracks. It took three minutes tops and we were at my future quarters. "Let's go lance corporal!"

"Yes, Sergeant." I replied as I stepped out of the 880, the military term of the Dodge pickup. After I unloaded my personal gear, we headed in the barracks to meet the company C.O.

I stood at attention as Captain Scott, gave me the command, "at ease Marine." I assumed the parade rest position. "Young man, I've heard a lot about you. Don't worry Marine it's good. I personally know your father son and let me tell you, he said to give you both barrels. But you know Marine, I'm a fair officer, and until I know otherwise, you have a clean state with me, that clear!"

"Yes, Sir!" I yelled thinking of my dad, he makes his presence known despite himself. "Dismissed!" I did an about face and exited the Captain's office. "Come on lance corporal, I'll show you your room! I eagerly followed the Sergeant, looking forward to ridding myself of my gear. We walked down the corridor of the immaculate and clean room. Activities were all around us as we headed toward my quarters. We came to a door and the Sergeant opened it, "that's your bunk over there next to the wall." I went over to the vacant wall locker next to the bed and opened it. Empty. I threw everything on the bunk. The Sergeant looked at me and stated, "look, you unpack and then report to the motor pool at 1300 hours."

"Aye, aye, Sergeant!" The Sergeant walked out of the room. I quickly began unpacking. I checked my watch, 9:45 a.m. and I still had to make it to chow. I was grateful that my sea bag and clothes carrier were organized or I'd have been in trouble. It took me under an hour to unpack. I had neatly arranged my utilities and my uniforms. Everything else I put in loosely so that I'd have access to it everyday. After squaring away everything, I ventured out of the semi squad bay. It appeared much nicer than Camp Foster. I noticed air conditioning ducts, which pleased me. I had heard that summers here on the Island got extremely hot. I had empathy for the marines at Camp Foster; they were at nature's mercy.

After asking directions to the chow hall, I ventured over there to eat. To my surprise, it was open. I went in and got my tray. I went on through the line and loaded up on everything I could get my hands on. Famished, I finished eating before the great influx of Marines would stampede on the dining facility at 1130 hours. Putting the rest of my gear in my footlocker before 1300 hours was my main objective. Deep in thought on my way back to the barracks, my mind drifted to my buddy, Jonah Crockett. We had been to truck driving school together aboard Camp Pendleton. Jonah had taken me under his wing so to speak and had guided me through the tough knocks of indoctrination to the Corps way of life. I had earned the nerve to openly communicate with the ladies; still I didn't quite measure up to the standards I desired. While home on leave, I had gone out several times with Louise, my child hood friend. Louise and I never took our clothes off, but we had a mutual attraction to each other. I mean back in Nebraska you normally picked a girl, get married and settle down. But with me joining the Marines, it put a whole new perspective on things.

Jonah was the only person I told that I did not sleep with a woman while on leave. I made Jonah swear not to tell my secret. Jonah, a New Yorker, absorbed my fear and patted me on the back and said, "stick with me Walters and you'll be fine." I trusted the likeable Marine. I dare not tell Jonah that my dad happened to be an Army Colonel. I didn't want to travel around the globe with my mom and dad, so I decided to live with my grandparents. My grandmother, an avid Catholic, made me vow that I'd fall in love before marriage. I promised grandma I'd do my best. Jonah, after listening to my experience one night after duty on Camp Pendleton, began calling me "Saint Walter," I cherished it.

One payday Jonah had talked me into going to Tijuana with him. At first, I was taken aback, but with Jonah's promises of hot sex, I gave in. My first orgasm was so explosive that I literally passed out. I remember the young lady trying to push me off of her. From that moment on I was hooked on tropical women. Sure, Louise was my first choice, but I had the whole world on a platter now and I'd taste it.

I decided to let my gear stay in the wall locker until after work. I'd go ahead and get to the motor pool early. I'd try and get a feel for things before the afternoon started. It would be a major part of my tour overseas, so I had to adjust to the work that went on at the motor pool. When I arrived at the company motor pool, there wasn't much activity going on, so I decided to look around. This would be a long tour from the looks of things; hopefully, I'd travel a lot so maybe I could stay away from this prison style affair. I went and took a look at the vehicles. In motor T. school I learned how to drive the tactical/commercial 5-ton vehicles. This certainly helped me to relax somewhat; I loved the sound the turbo made when the vehicle was going. The whistling turbo gave the truck the big rig feel. After learning about the troop carriers, the tractors might be in the works, but I knew that would take time and effort. I hung around for eternity it seemed. I had begun to perspire, my uniform felt sticky. It was September, but one couldn't tell by the weather. The Island's proximity betrayed the weather. I figured it to be chilly, but what the heck, I'd deal with it.

The company slowly began trickling in. I quickly went to the shop to see what the plans would be for me my first day on the job. I stood waiting for formation perhaps 15 minutes. "Fall in!" Sergeant Larson boomed. I quickly ran to my place in the rear of the formation. "Listen up Marines, all of you who have runs today get going when formation is over. Let's work hard and safe Marines, fall out!" Everyone splintered in their perspective assignments. Lance Corporal Walters, front and center!" I quickly ran to the Sergeant and locked my body. "Yes, Sergeant!" I yelled exhibiting my Marine Corps training. "How did you get promoted so fast?"

"I graduated boot camp private first class and I earned lance corporal by being the highest score in Motor Transport School."

"Good. I hope it sticks to you Marine, promotions come hard in Motor T, keep your bearing."

"Yes Sergeant!"

"Listen, Walters, what I want you to go with Private Curtis over to consolidated Motor Transport and get your license stamped. You can't drive on the streets of Okinawa without it. Clear!"

"Aye, Aye, Sergeant Larson!" Private Curtis, a homely, dark green Marine, but well built, motioned for me to follow him, which I did. "Come on Walters, it's right around the corner." Quietly I followed the amiable non-rate over to Consolidated Motors.

Once we got there, I had to take a written test, which took ten minutes and of course I passed with flying colors. As we walked back to the motor pool, private Curtis led me away from the shop and out into the yard. "Walters, you ever drive one of these babies?"

"Yeah, I trained with them at Camp Pendleton."

"Oh, so you're a Hollywood Marine?"

"Indeed, I am Curtis. What about you?"

"Paris Island babe, uurrahh!" I laughed at the gung-ho Marine. He appeared to be highly motivated. "So, tell me Curtis, where are we going?"

"Well, if you must know we are going to show you a few bases."

"Curtis, you mean we are going to spend the afternoon riding around?"

"You catch on quick Walters. You College educated?"

"Yes, I have my Associate Degree. You?"

"Three years at the University of Georgia, second baseman. I wanted to go pro, but I got in a bit of trouble." Curtis looked wearily at me as though he told the story a thousand times and dreaded going into it again. I told him to tell it anyway with my expression. We both got into the truck and before he started the engine Curtis continued. "Well, I met this white chick and we hit it off. We were in love my man and we decided to go steady. Only problem was that her dad wasn't real keen on me being with his little girl. I was kicked off the team."

"Well, you could have gone pro Curtis."

"Not that simple my man. I wasn't the greatest. Maybe triple A, but I had to many issues with sliders and curve balls. I still needed time to develop." Curtis looked over at me trying to pull a question out. He went on anyway. "I figured I'd do the next best thing, become a U.S. Marine."

"You can always play ball for the Corps, can't you?"

"That's behind me now. All I want to do is be with my sweetie and be one of the world's finest."

"How about your girl?'

"She works at the exchange."

"She's here!" I exclaimed extremely surprised.

"Yes, I signed on for a three-year tour because my girl didn't want to be without me." Curtis looked over at me with confidence. I saw him in a different light now. A handsome man with the salesman's eyes reassured me about his intentions. "So, tell me Curtis, how did her father not liking you get you kicked off the team?"

"Look, son, Georgia and the good ole boys are like glue man. A black kid had better mind his manners there or he could come up missing. Luckily, I had enough pull there that they only dropped me off the team. I've seen worse happen." I refrained from answering Curtis. Lord knows the trouble blacks experienced in the United States and I didn't want to add my two cents.

"Tell me Walters, what made you enlist in the Corps?"

"Two things Curtis, boredom and women."

"Women! You seem like a man who can handle himself amongst

the ladies fairly easy."

"Looks can be deceiving my man especially in my case. No, Curtis, I have been one who want to discover what makes a woman tick besides the wham bam thank you ma'am!" Curtis eyed me, "Are you religious Walters?"

"Not to the extreme, but I did promise my grandmother."

"Give it time Walters, you'll be kicking the doors down for a piece." Curtis laughed, a very deep laugh that shook the inside of the 5-ton. "You're probably right Curtis, knowing you have experienced marriage and what not."

"It's not that Walters. It's the fact that testosterone is a powerful thing and in Okinawa with your being unrestrained something's got to give." Curtis wheeled the cargo truck toward a military base. As we drove, I finally realized that we were on the opposite side of the road. "This is Camp Foster, Walters, you probably know that."

"Yes, as a matter of fact I do Curtis, but what was the base we passed already?"

"Oh, that's Fatima Air Wing. You won't get many runs there. Listen Walters; you'll probably get most of your runs to Camp Hansen or Camp Foster. That's how it works with H&S Company."

"How long have you been on the Rock Curtis?"

"For six months Walters; time gets by quick. Curtis then seemed to concentrate on where he was driving. "Pay attention Walters, there will be plenty of times you'll be called here, got it!"

"Got it Curtis!" I began watching numbers on the buildings. We drove for ten minutes before Curtis stopped the vehicle. "Listen, Walters, we're here to pick up some new bees and take them to Camp Hansen. I want you to make sure everyone is properly seated and put on the safety strap. We don't want any accidents here; safety's always first. Believe me Walters, some strange things have happened that can't be explained." Curtis gave me a strange look.

"Why are you only a private Curtis?"

"Well, Walters, one thing about the corps, you'll learn quickly, easy come easy go. I lost it by falling asleep on duty. I had earned Corporal and I had it six months, and then just like that you know, I was tired and on late duty and blanked out. Next thing I know the Sergeant of the guard woke me up and before you knew it my stripes were stripped off." We stopped the conversation as a grubby looking Staff Sergeant peered out of a door. "You here for Staff Sergeant Jackson?"

"Yes, we're here for Marines going to Camp Hansen." Curtis seemed confident and assured, maybe being a non-commissioned officer, helped him, either way he handled himself professionally.

"Driver, stand by, they will be ready shortly."

"Aye, aye, Staff Sergeant." Curtis made sure the vehicle was safe. I took note so when my turn came, I'd be ready. "You smoke Walters?"

"Never touched them."

"Well, I'm going to take a smoke break." Curtis got out of the truck and lit one up. I sat in the vehicle and waited.

I hadn't heard from Crockett since I left Pendleton. He, too, was Okinawa bound, and he may be with these Marines. I thought of my dad. He had said he'd come to Okinawa in time to visit me before my tour was up. Knowing dad, he'd inform H&S co. Commander and they'd no doubt get in touch with me. I surveyed the area. This, as ancient looking, as the Corps could get stood huge. I knew it did not have a lot of comforts, but the year of today being 1980, one never knew the changes that could come about. Maybe Camp Foster just may become technologically advanced. Curtis opened the truck door; "here they come Walters, get ready!" I jumped out of the truck and helped Curtis let the rear tailgate down. As the troops loaded up, I searched for Jonah Crockett, no such luck. After the Marines boarded the 5-ton, Curtis got behind the wheel and I rode shotgun. "Well, Walters, we're headed to Camp Hansen on the north side of the Island. Check out the scenery on the way over, it might surprise you man!"

"What are you trying to say Curtis?"

"I mean for the most part most Marines want to get to know Okinawan women, but as far as I'm concerned, they go about it the wrong way."

"I still don't follow you, Curtis."

"Listen Walters, try and get a decent girl here, that's what I'm saying. Forget about the whores." I contemplated the word, "forget the whores." No way. I'd for certain try the whores. For once I didn't have anyone looking over my shoulders. I could explore my horizons and find out exactly what sexuality was all about. "You're mighty quiet Walters."

"Just thinking about what you said friend."

"I'm not trying to run your life or anything, but I've seen the streets of Okinawa ruin Marines Walters, I mean, they turn to alcohol or find themselves arrested, or they just plain get the wrong girl. Know what I mean?"

"Yes, Curtis, I understand you completely, but I'll take my chances alright."

"Just be smart Marine."

"I will Curtis, I assure you." Curtis relaxed and seemed to concentrate on driving. I begin sightseeing. For an Island, Okinawa had very interesting sights. As we rode, I listened to the turbo scream. Although a governor limited the 5-tons, they still ran with power.

The ocean, in its entire splendor looked magnificent. The bluish green water sparkled as though one could reach out and drink it. I had to admit, the Okinawans were a creative people. The buildings and homes were constructed in a way that looked good and was space saving. I tried to observe the many well-dressed young girls who shuffled to and fro. I couldn't get over the fact that the Island contained so many attractive young women. By the time we arrived at Camp Hansen, I had looked forward to stretching my legs. I mean at six feet two, it could get quite cramped sitting in the truck. I loved the breeze though, it seemed to blow right threw my high and tight. The expressway was unusual, not much traffic and it helped get us to Hansen faster. As Curtis wheeled the truck toward the barracks, someone yelled for him to stop the vehicle. "Right here driver!" Curtis expertly stopped the vehicle and I went and let the tailgate down. The dozen or so Marines quickly filed out and ran over to the chow hall. After everyone had vacated the vehicle, Curtis inquired as to whether or not I wanted to eat chow. "Why not Curtis, I'm hungry anyway." Curtis parked the vehicle in a secure area and we slowly walked to the chow hall line and waited for the Marine Corps chow, eagerly hoping some would be around by the time we got in.

CHAPTER TWO
CAMEKO

I had been on Okinawa for two weeks, and let me tell you, routine is learned fast around here. I had begun to drive off Base, my first run was to pick up Marines from Camp Foster and then bring them back to Camp Kinser. The roads were such that the 5-ton took up the whole lane. The Okinawans, driving mostly compact cars, whizzed by me anyway. I had heard that the roads were made out of corrals. I didn't debate with the news, but with amused skepticism I accepted it. Another little tidbit that caught my attention is that the sewage system was about a foot or so deep and ran parallel to the road. Maybe that's why they call it the Rock; impenetrable being the factor.

During my first run to Camp Foster, I almost wrecked. While observing female goodies I nearly rear-ended a street bus. Thank goodness for air brakes. My Motor T, Commanding Officer, appeared to like me. He even wanted me to drive for Headquarters C.O. if need be. I didn't necessarily want that job, but orders were orders. Jonah had finally

Whisper Alley

arrived on Okinawa. He being stationed over at Camp Hansen. He wrote me a letter explaining the conditions of Camp Hansen, very few if any Women Marines. I chuckled; being aware that here on Kinser WM's was everywhere. We had a large WM barracks that housed hundreds of the felines. Maybe in time I'd meet one.

Jonah had made plans for me to come to Camp Hansen and meet him Saturday. Being that today was Wednesday, I had given him word the previous Monday that I'd come. I'd take the Base Bus all the way over if need be or try and use public transportation. I still felt befuddled trying to make sense of the Okinawan language. It sounded as though the Okinawans were singing. I chuckled at the thought, people actually communicating by singing. I became serious when I thought of West Side story

Today, I was to stay at the shop and do preventative maintenance. I had learned a bit about keeping the vehicle safe. There wasn't a whole lot to do but grease and check the batteries and fluids. While getting tools I went into the mechanic section. These Marines kept it all going; sure, we did the hauling, but the mechanics were the glue. Sergeant Larsen spotted me nosing, "Walters, what's up?"

"Getting a wrench Sergeant Larsen."

"Okay, make sure you don't take all day!"

"Yes Sergeant!" He reminded me of the Drill Instructors when I was in Boot Camp, but Larsen wasn't that cut of a Marine. He looked scrappy and all with the tight build and the leathery face, but he didn't carry himself in a Drill sergeant's manner. Larsen appeared to be a devoted family man who wanted to serve his Country. I respected him for that. I went ahead and checked out the wrench and went on back to my truck. Today for some reason lance Corporal Charles Tucker, an Arizona native, wanted to school me in the art of buying sex. "Listen, Walters, you can't go to Whisper Alley on payday man, it's too many people trying to buy snatch."

"Okay, Tucker, what's the plan." I looked over at Tucker who was sweating profusely. It was after 2:00 p.m. and I knew he hadn't had a drink yet, but Tucker could be deceptive. "Walters, you have to go right before payday. It's empty and sometimes you can get a deal."

"What kind of deal Tucker?"

"Don't you know Walters? Boy, you are wet behind the ears."

"No, I don't know Tucker." Flabbergasted, but nonetheless I waited for Tucker to respond. Finally he said, "don't tell anyone, but you can trade liquor, cigarettes, and other goods for a short time among other things."

"What's a short time Tucker?" I don't know why I said that because Tucker, lost all sense of himself. He must have laughed for five minutes. Finally Pfc Curtis, laughing as well came over. "Walters, look, man, a short time is purchasing sex for 2 or 3 minutes until you have an orgasm. But don't drink first. They won't let you screw them. It will take too long."

"How do you know Curtis?"

"I get around Walters." the twelve or so Marines drivers all heard my ignorance and made fun of me. I took it in stride though knowing I had learned a valuable lesson. Liquor for sex, I couldn't resist that possibility. By the time formation was called everyone knew of my lack of knowledge of Whisper Alley.

That evening, after chow, I decided to work out at the base gym. The thing I liked about Camp Kinser was not only that it happened to be an old Army Base, but also the gym had class. There were several places that I really liked the Sauna and the weight room. Tonight, I wanted the basics. Pushups, maybe 5 sets of twenty, 80 sit-ups and some leg work. I didn't feel like running because at 8:00 tonight lance corporal Tucker was taking me out for a night on the town.

I finished my workout in less than an hour. I showered at the gym and put on my street clothes. I met Tucker at the Barracks, "hey, Walters, what do you say?"

"I'm ready Tucker."

"So am I." Tucker said arching his already cocked eyebrow. Although it didn't arouse any suspicion on my part. Tucker, all six feet of him appeared to be in control. I knew he drank heavy, but he handled himself well enough. We headed for the base enlisted club where the taxi's awaited Marines going out in town. "Listen, Walters, we need a plan. We can't go out without watching each other's back. I'm not against blacks Walters, but some of them will rob you if you're not careful." I soaked in Tucker's knowledge. I observed Tucker as we walked. A well-built Marine, and with his slight bulge around the midsection gave away his weakness, alcohol. Tucker probably worked out during company physical training. He appeared to be able to handle himself, yet he had the mentality of most Southerners. "You okay Walters?"

"Yes, Tucker, just deep in thought."

"About niggers?" Tucker chuckled.

"Listen, Tucker," I growled, I know you might not like blacks, but some of them are good men and don't deserve to be thought of as niggers!"

"But, Walters, they were slaves you know. And majority of them don't have proper upbringing. They think whites owe them for their hard work during captivity."

"You're the expert in reparations Tucker?"

"Now wait a minute Walters, what's stuck up your craw?"

"It's just that I don't like putting people down. I want everyone to be treated equal at least to me personally."

"I understand Walters, but what about our plan?"

"Tucker, if we get robbed or in a fight don't worry, we'll handle it. And I'll cover you, but don't drink heavily Tucker or you'll play right into a thug's hands."

"So, you agree that blacks are thugs?"

"No, I agree that any man who robs his fellow brother in arms regardless of his race is a thug."

"My dad told me never trust a nigger, but I learned in Boot Camp to respect a black who are genuine."

"Anyway Tucker, some whites steal too."

"At this level Walters?"

"Sure, Tucker, why do you think that only blacks break the law?"

"I'm certain whites do, maybe even Japanese, but blacks are known to do it."

"The media has a lot to do with that Tucker." Tucker grew quiet as we came up on the Base enlisted club. Tucker flagged down a taxi. The cab driver rushed to us. "Where too," the driver asked in broken English. His efforts were almost amazing. "I takka you to mommason okay?"

"Gate Two Street Honcho!" Tucker semi yelled jumping into the cab. I quickly followed Tucker's lead and slid into the back seat next to Tucker. "Okay, Gate Two Street, okay G.I."

"Yeah, and put on some rock and roll Honcho."

"Okay." The cab driver popped in some Pink Floyd. Surprised I relaxed and prepared for the ride. Always impressed with the view of Camp Kinser with the Ocean staring at you every day. I loved the power the seductive way the waters splashed on the shore.

We rode in silence for a few minutes then Tucker whispered in my ear. "Walters, just stick with me and follow my lead."

"Sure Tucker, this is my first time out here. Come to think of it I am a little leery."

"I know the feeling Walters, I've been on the Island for almost a year and I come out here once a month, you know, to keep the system from over charging."

"Ha, that's cute Tucker, so have you ever found a real girlfriend?"

"Are you serious!" Tucker looked at me incredulously. The cab driver spoke out, "you wanna go someplace else!"

"No, Honcho, just Gate two."

"Okay, G.I."

"Listen, Walters, you don't want to fall in love out here these women are not the marrying type."

"So, you mean whores Tucker?"

"Exactly Walters!" I knew deep down inside I wanted a young whore. A feeling deep down inside of me had been lit now that I lived as a Marine, and a prostitute in my book could be trained if you treated her right. Tucker didn't speak anymore. I respected Tucker, but I knew he did not share my views on women. Tucker wanted the traditional woman. Who cooked, cleaned, and waited on him. I wanted the wild stallion that despite herself wanted to be caught and put in a cage. Maybe it was the women in Tijuana or my dreaming of sex with foreign women. In any case I was hooked.

The cab driver pulled up to Gate 2 Street. "I takka you back to Base G.I.?"

"Yeah, in about an hour, we'll flag you down Honcho."

"Okay G.I." We got out of the cab. The Street teamed with activities. There were Clubs and music blaring everywhere. Military personnel flooded the area. Tucker led me into a small Street. "I'm going to have a few drinks Walters, you game?"

"Sure, why not Tucker." We followed the Street until we came out on another Street with still more Clubs. "This is where the action is kid. Tucker led me to a door with a short but stout looking dark Okinawan man yelling, "come inside, we have girls, drinks, and show!"

"Come on Walters! Let's get inside before the crowd comes!"

"What! A crowd Tucker, I thought we came for sex!" Confused, I rushed in the Club with Tucker anyway. The maze of lights in the Japanese language had triggered my ignorance of things. As we sat down a waitress quickly came over. "You wanna drinkey?"

"Yeah, sweetheart, I want two Purple Haze please." Tucker patted the woman on the rear end, she giggled and waltzed away toward the Bar. "Hey, Tucker, what are you doing man, you want to get us in trouble!"

"Relax Walters, I'm paying her for sex every now and then." I became instantly erect. "Hey do you think…"

"Forget it, Walters." Tucker gave me a sly grin, "she is a very expensive piece." I observe the waitress. Nice; she was slim with small breast, but she had a nice overall appearance.

Her cute face belied her years. She had on a cute little light blue mini skirt, which went well with her halter-top. She had tight but small breast that went well with her ponytail, which almost went to her shoulders. She looked a little bit like the Hispanic women I met over in Tijuana only smaller. I would say at least thirty, but who cared, hot sex was hot sex. The waitress brought the drinks over. "Hey Cameko, this is my buddy, Walters."

"Do you have a first name?" The waitress asked in surprisingly good English.

"Yeah, but only for those that know me well young lady."

"Okay, you and me, we good friends?"

"If you like Cameko."

"Okay, I get off work in two hours you come back?"

"As a matter of fact, I'll wait here for you dear."

"Oh, no, you drink too much, you go and come back later."

"Alright, anything you say Cameko." She smiled and looked at Tucker.

"It's fine Cameko, I'm going home soon anyway."

"When you leave Okinawa Tucker?"

"Oh, in about two months."

"Okay, I take both of you tonight. Me toxon horny." We both laughed with me catching the last word. Tucker pondered a bit. "No Cameko, you bring friend for me, I want to try a new girl tonight."

"Okay, I bring friend. Meet us here in maybe one hour, okay?"

"Yes Cameko." We both drank the sweet smooth Purple Haze. As we left, the dozen or so men in the Club eyed us suspiciously. When we were outside, I said, "hey Tucker, you think she'll be there?"

"Of course Walters, she will treat you right if you pay her well."

"How much?"

"At least a hundred dollars each time you sleep with her." I gave Tucker a quizzical look. "Damn, Tucker, you really spoiled her."

"Look, Walters, she's clean and she only sleeps with certain guys. You're lucky she likes you. As a matter of fact, you're the first person besides me that she's taken too."

"Really?"

"Yeah, most guys come in too strong. Come on let me show you Whisper Alley." We walked back toward gate 2 Street. I hadn't paid much attention, but the Purple Haze hit me like a sledgehammer. "Damn, Tucker, what's in the drink?"

"Ever heard of the song Purple Haze Walters."

"Yes Tucker, I have."

"Excuse me while I kiss the sky. Come on you'll be all right, but I see that Cameko was right. You probably would have really tied one on if we had stayed in the club."

"By the way what's the name of the Club Tucker?" My speech had slurred somewhat. "Osake or something of that nature, I'm not sure, but I'll never forget it." We arrived back on Gate 2 Street. Still, activity flourished only now it had begun to subside a bit. "What now Tucker?"

"Come on, I'll show you Whisper Alley."

"Great let's go!" We went back in the small roadway near Gate 2. When we came on Whisper Alley, I knew it immediately. "This is it isn't it, Tucker."

"Yeah, now do you see why I pay so much."

"Well, I still will try it, but I expected much more glamour."

"Welcome to reality my man." We cautiously walked down the darkened raggedy looking strip. Americans were shuffling about and some were finishing up with the Japanese hookers. I don't know if it was the liquor or the Alley, but for the first time I smelled sulfur along with the sewer. God forbid that it the smell came from the illicit sex, yet I knew that it heightened my desire.

"Hey, Walters, you want to try it?" Tucker tried to steer me toward one door in particular, "no Tucker, I'll wait for Cameko alright!"

"What do you have to lose Walters, it's just pussy." Tucker laughed as he let go of my arm. "Why don't we walk to the other end and try a few of the other Bars on the strip."

"Look, Tucker, I want something to eat, I'm famished."

"Me, too, let's go over to Lido's and then we'll go over to talk with Cameko." We took the walk over to the small fish shack. The fish was excellent. Lido, an African American, no doubt military, had found his niche over here on the Island. After the sumptuous meal, we headed back toward Cameko's Club. To our surprise Cameko was outside waiting with another female. "Hey, Cameko, how long have you been waiting?"

"Not long I got off early, I wanted some American love."

"Well, Walters, it seems like Cameko likes you." Cameko took me by the arm, "let's go to my place." Tucker, the ladies' man that he is took Cameko's friend by the hand and followed us. We walked in relative silence. Having a girl on your arms this side of town was rare indeed. Even though I had only been here for a short time, I could see the disparity. I knew that not only did you need money; you had to have the right view or just be fortunate enough to woo the females. Tucker broke the silence, "Taxi!" he yelled. The taxi quickly stopped. "I takka you to Base?"

"No, Honcho, to the hotel down the street."

"You like Okinawan girl G.I.?" Tucker giggled and patted the driver on the back, "yeah, Honcho, very beautiful." Everyone chuckled and seemed to settle down. The cab driver got to the hotel quickly. We all stepped out. Surprisingly Cameko paid. As we got inside, Tucker began kissing his friend. Cameko smiled and said, "Tucker is horny, you horny Walters?" I put my hand on Cameko's shoulder, "I think, but we'll see later in the room, okay?"

"Okay." The clerk, an older man, who appeared to care less about business here, he had probably saw so many couples coming here to have illicit sex. Then again there was no telling how long he had saw Cameko and Tucker over the course of time. "You pay twenty dollars now and when you leave!" I detested some resentment in the ole fellow. Cameko begin talking in Japanese. They talked for at least 5 minutes, and then Cameko finally put a twenty on the counter. Tucker quickly put up another twenty. "Okay, this is good, you stay long time."

"Thanks, poppasan." As we headed upstairs, my erection throbbed. I couldn't wait to see Cameko naked. Tucker was practically raping his friend, as we were alone upstairs. She giggled inviting the pawing Tucker to continue. As Tucker fumbled to open the door, Cameko whispered in my ear. "Tucker is always horny, I like nice guy you know, you nice guy, let's just talk okay, no make love." I couldn't believe it, no sex! What the hell, but I feebly agreed. "Okay, Cameko, we'll get to know each other better." I knew Cameko was testing me. My instincts told me that she wanted to be serious. We both lay in bed, "okay, what do you want to talk about Cameko?" Cameko snuggled up next to me. I involuntarily jerked. My penis tore through my underwear. I could fell the wetness. "Walters, you like Okinawan girl?"

"Yeah, Cameko, I think you are a nice girl."

"I work in Bar Walters, I'm not nice girl." Cameko buried her head in my chest and softly sobbed. "Hey, don't cry Cameko, I think you are a very nice girl."

"Would you marry me, Walters?" Without hesitating I said yes. Knowing had I said anything else, I would have lost her. "I like you Walters, let's be friends and you still give me money right now."

"How much Cameko?"

"One hundred dollars."

"Okay, Cameko, I'll give you the money now let's just lay here in each other's arms and relax." I couldn't believe I said that.

"Okay, Walters;" I began kissing Cameko around the eyes. She responded by relaxing a bit. "We kiss, okay, but no make love."

"Cameko, I want you to trust in me, I'll treat you right." I began caressing Cameko rubbing her up and down her shoulders to her midsection. I was careful not to pull up her mini skirt although I was dying to see what color her panties were. We kissed, light kisses, for I knew Cameko was no virgin, but we were relative strangers and to blow this opportunity I'd never forgive myself. "You make me feel good Walters."

"Hmm, hmm." I continued stroking Cameko. By now she had closed her eyes. I studied my Okinawan beauty. She had dark skin and her almond shaped eyes went well with her small nose and mouth. I loved her small moist lips. I'd say half an hour later someone was banging on the door. "Come on Walters, we have to get back to Base!" It was Tucker. Cameko abruptly sat up. "Okay, we go now, you meet me at my Club next week, Monday okay, Walters?"

"Okay, Cameko." We both got out of bed. Cameko looked at my erection. She smiled and touched it. "You big American man." I embraced my friend, "I'll see you Monday."

"Okay." Quickly I reached into my pocket and counted five twenties. I usually kept yen for taxis or other needs. Cameko took the money and tucked it in her bra. I kissed her on her lips one last time and headed for the door. Tucker practically kicked the door in. "Come on Walters, it's getting late!" I observed Tucker for any feelings of jealousy he may have had for me. He appeared to be snug and self-assured. "Where's Kim?" Tucker replied, "she left a bit ago, we didn't hit it off to well. After we screwed, she wanted two hundred and I only gave her fifty, it's all I had on me man!" Cameko who had came out of the room didn't challenge Tucker, but she quickly departed but not before squeezing my hand. Tucker gave me the once over and looked at Cameko's backside. "Let's go friend, we have to work tomorrow." In the cab Tucker drilled me. "How was she Walters?"

"Great, Tucker, just great." Tucker studied me.

"Did she ask about money Walters?"

"Well, she likes to see if she can count on you if she needs too, you know, she'll only sleep with you if she can trust the way you treat her."

"Is she sincere Tucker?"

"Very, believe me when I say it Walters, I slept with her three times and then she started talking of commitment, but not I, I have a blond vixen waiting for me in Phoenix, and I'm going to marry her."

"Well, does Cameko want money or what Tucker?" I studied Tucker intently as he answered. 'I think she wants out of Okinawa. She doesn't have a lot of family. Don't mention it to her, but Cameko is an orphan that works for the Yakuza."

"What the hell is the Yakuza?"

"Listen, Walters, never ask about the Yakuza, never!" Tucker grabbed my arm and looked seriously into my eyes. I could see the raw fear. "But what will I do about Cameko Tucker?"

"Walters just roll with the punches and try not to fall in love. If you do get her out quickly and without much noise." I begin to see that Tucker was more than an empty-headed alcoholic. He was a concerned man who knew the ropes and knew when to pull punches. "What about you and Cameko Tucker?"

"Tonight my friend, you have been anointed with Cameko."

"So, this was a setup."

"No, she told me to find her a nice G.I. and I picked you."

"You sly dog you!" I playfully punched Tucker on the arm he smiled and looked away. The cab driver spoke out, "where you go G.I.?"

"Camp Kinser, Honcho, Camp Kinser." I saw how Tucker watched the cab driver for it seemed like a sign to see if the cab driver understood what it was we were just discussing. The cab driver never let on.

That night I tossed and turned. On the one hand Cameko seemed like a good person, but everything was shady. Tucker not telling me prior and Cameko asking for money on our first date didn't set well with me. In America, a woman usually waited until marriage or serious commitment to lower the boom. I hoped Cameko wanted to see if I was sincere. I didn't want to be used.

And Tucker talking of Yakuza, I didn't know what to think. As I tried to fall asleep, I dreamed of dragons and serpents. When I woke up that Thursday morning everything was a fog. People, places, lies, romance, all intertwined to create my interpretation of what I was into. I hurriedly went to the showers, my towel concealing my genitals. Although frightened, the dreams caused an explosion. My discharge was so great that if there was a thunderous explosion I wasn't aware of it.

CHAPTER THREE
JONAH'S TEAR

That Saturday morning, I found myself at Camp Hansen. Not too bad if I had to say so myself, I had hitched a ride from Pfc Curtis, who had a run there early this morning. My pal Jonah was surprised to see me so early but he let me in despite everything. There was an empty rack in the small squad bay, so I bunked in it the rest of the morning. Later, Jonah had awakened me, "rise and shine Marine, it's time to get some chow!"

"What time is it?" I groggily asked, slowly rising to my feet.

"It's 8:30 in the morning Walters, and I'm starved so let's hit it!" I stood and balanced myself. I didn't realize how tired I was. The activities of Marine life wore on you as time went on, but sleep was something I could never get enough of. We headed to the chow hall to get breakfast. "How do you like the Rock so far Walters?"

"Well, to be perfectly honest Crockett, I like it very much, I've even met me a girl."

"Oh, yeah, and how'd you manage to do that so soon?" Jonah nudged me and gave me a knowing look.

"I had help. A fellow Marine introduced me to her."

"Is she pretty?"

"She'll do. Anyway Jonah, I want to explore my options and this young lady is one of them."

"Walters, you have to remember that this isn't America by any stretch of the imagination. Japanese women live by a different creed."

"Well, if it isn't Mr. Know it all strutting his stuff."

"I'm serious Walters, you can become so involved that you can lose track of everything else and become sidetracked."

"So tell me Jonah, how did you become such an expert?"

"My brother married an Okinawan." That did it. Jonah proved right then and there that he knew not only knew the culture of women over here, he probably had a lot of insight about relationships. "So how does your brother get along with his wife?"

"Oh, they get along well. To well for that matter, my poor brother doesn't have time for anything else except good ole Yumi. She has his nose open so wide a regiment could belly crawl through it and he'd never notice."

"Do you like her Jonah?"

"Sure, but she never talks. Every time she and my brother visit home, she sits there staring at my brother."

"Where did they meet Jonah?"

"In a night club in mainland, she happened to be a stripper." We both laughed at that one. I had to admit Okinawan girl's whatever occupation they held were certainly sharp enough to land an American whether by charm or physical attraction. Whatever the case, the attractiveness of the girls remained unquestionable. As I walked with Jonah to the chow hall, we observed the long chow line. "Damn, I thought we'd beat the crowd." Jonah said a bit perturbed.

"Well, you want to eat out in town?"

"Are you serious! Outside the gate!"

"Yes."

"Be serious Walters, this isn't your part of town."

"Is it that bad Jonah?"

"Yep. I've been out once and let me tell you, it's the pits."

"Well, we'd better get in line then." We took the last place in line and bit our tongue as we waited for breakfast.

After breakfast we went to the U.S.O. club on Base. I noticed Jonah was withdrawn now, not the outgoing confident person I knew him to be. When we didn't have people right next to us I asked him, "What seems to be the trouble Jonah?" Jonah tried to feign denial, so I said, "come on Jonah you're nothing like you used to be in the States, now what is it?" Jonah looked right at me and practically whispered, "Walters, thank god you're not stationed here!"

"What do you mean Jonah?"

"This is the real Marine Corps Walters." I tried to understand.

"Are you saying that you're going to combat?"

"What I'm saying is that this side of the Island the Corps is all business."

"So are you saying you can't handle it?" I asked a bit concerned.

"I don't know, I think I can, but I'm getting the hell out of here when my year is up."

"I see. Don't do anything stupid my friend; you have too much riding here. Handle this and you've earned your medal." Jonah sighed and motioned for us to leave the building. "What do you want to do now Jonah?"

"Let's walk outside the gate. I might by some trinkets or whatever."

"Sounds good to me." We headed for the main gate. Jonah, whatever made him change, seemed to be leathery now. Maybe he had a point, the mental edge that we heard of about the Corps was honed right here. Noticing the absence of women I felt for Jonah. He had always managed to find a way to mingle with the females. Hopefully he'd pull out this funk it appeared he was in. The Gate guards looked upon us curiously as we passed them. Possibly the time, it was before 10 a. m.

Jonah, noticing the scene spoke out as we were out of ear shot, "things don't start happening around here until evening Walters, don't let it bother you, they are just bored."

"If you say so Jonah." We got in the town and observed the happenings. There were a few shop owners out haggling and trying to make bargains. This was nothing like Gate 2, but it was just as sleazy. I immediately felt that attraction. Nebraska, for the most part happened to be a nice place, but I had a different feel for it. Louise and I were attracted to each other out of obligation rather than feelings. As Jonah and I walked we saw the Okinawan tailors plying their wares. Jonah, dressed in jeans and a long sleeve white cotton shirt, was casual to say the least, but he was comfortable looking. I tried to read Jonah as we walked, but he watched me closely too, so I was limited to what I could do. Finally, Jonah decided to go to a building, which was a bit deteriorated, but had life in it. We both entered, it was smelly, stale beer and cigarettes. It was dark and drabby even in the bright morning sunshine. I immediately thought of illicit sex. An old Okinawan woman, smoking a cigarette greeted us. "Come in Marines, what can I do for you?"

"Two beers Nason." Jonah yelled out. He led me to a seat, "come on Walters, we might as well enjoy it while we can." When we sat down, I studied my friend. "What seems to be bugging you, Jonah?" Jonah looked at me square in the eye.

"Walters, I got my girl pregnant while I was home on leave and she seems to think I'll do twenty years in the Corps and leave her and the baby in New York."

"I, see." So that's what rattled Mr. Jonah Crockett. I had assumed he was a man of steel. I guess now I knew otherwise. Jonah took a long swallow of Budweiser before continuing. "Walters, she is a school teacher, I can't lose her man, I was her first, never mind that she's black!" I practically stood up in my chair,

"Black!"

"Yes, a beautiful educated girl who did not grow up in the slums. I met her at the library in Upstate New York. I was doing research on the military and she was studying for her B.A.. We hit it off and I fell in love Walters."

"Why didn't you marry her Jonah?"

"Walters, you don't know black women that well do you. If you haven't forgot, I'm a white man who's not highly educated, I still don't see how Monique took me, but she did Walters and now I could lose her." Jonah buried his face in his hands. He didn't cry, but I could see that he was in great pain. "Jonah, you're a hell of a man, any girl would be lucky to have you she'll wait." I tried to convince my friend. "Walters, she said that she wouldn't keep the baby and that she won't wait for me." I remained silent, damn; I didn't know what to say to my friend. This one was tough. I took a swallow of beer and waited for Jonah to respond. It took ten minutes. "Listen, Walters, I've contemplated suicide!" I refused to comment, let him get it out maybe that would soothe his nerves. I could see the pain etched in his ever-quivering hands. We both drank our beers in silence. I motioned for two more. They quickly came. We were the only customers at this point. I looked at my watch, not even 11:00 a.m. Finally Jonah spoke, "Walters, I'm not killing myself but I'm trying to arrange for Monique to come to Okinawa. I've got about ten thousand in the bank and if we marry, I'll have her and the child with me."

"This is good Jonah, keep working at it, don't give up!"

"I won't my friend." Jonah took my hand and said, "Walters, you know you're the first person I could safely tell about wanting to kill myself and not freak out. Thanks man."

"Awe Jonah, that's what friends are for." We both grabbed the ice-cold beers.

We sat there for three hours. We had drunk a six-pack and it cost us $20 dollars. I had a pretty good buzz, still no other customers. "What do you say we leave this joint Walters?"

"Alright, let's walk around a bit, I want to see what this side of town has to offer."

"Clarksville is alright when you're drunk, what does Kinser have to offer Walters?"

"It's a world apart my friend and I have not even been to the Island Capital, Naha."

"I see. So are there a lot of women in those parts?"

"Jonah, let me tell you, there are thousands, but it helps if you can speak the language."

"That's a gimme Walters." Jonah stood which was the sign for us to leave. The bartender waved as we departed the murky club. Jonah appeared to feel a bit better, but I could tell his thoughts raced through his mind. "Walters, do you think a girl from the Big Apple could live here on Okinawa?"

"Honestly Jonah, no, I don't think so."

"What if she worked teaching school and we could save a few bucks and really live good in the States once we got back."

"Jonah, don't listen to me, just get her here so that you'll have her. It's a damn shame she's putting you through this!"

"Any other girl Walters, and I'd tell her to have the abortion and do whatever, but Monique, she's a doll. I feel that not even another black man could come between us, she's that genuine." I didn't comment on the naïve Jonah. Did he really believe that? Boy, love could do strange things to people, but Jonah! We walked toward the Base Gate. Jonah, always the adventuresome one, plus with the beers boiling inside of him suggested that we go into one of the several cathouses of Clarksville. "How about it Walters?

"Well, Jonah, I don't know, it's not that I don't want to but to be honest I have an engagement next week that I want to be ready for."

"Are you going to screw her Walters?" I looked at Jonah before I answered he had some nerve. "If I can Jonah!"

"Well, I remember a certain Marine at Camp Pendleton who didn't know which way was up."

"I've changed since then man!" Jonah took it in stride while we headed toward the whorehouse. "I'm ready to explode Walters, and besides my girl Monique won't mind, she's too busy making me miserable." Jonah entered the building. I stood outside, daring not to follow suit. I didn't want to risk losing Cameko right now. To pay for as it's called a short time, I wouldn't risk it. Jonah though, had little regard for my feelings. He being from New York accepted life differently than most. I imagine he had seen so much human carnage that it was easy to be calloused to simple things. He falling in love like that, Monique must have been something special.

I decided to look at some of the wares that the local Okinawan salesmen were selling. China dishes, clothing, music, they had a bit of everything. Oddly enough today I was not in the mood to haggle or carry anything. I waited for maybe 15 minutes and decided to go see what Jonah was up to. No sooner had I got to the door Jonah burst out of it. His jeans were still unbuttoned and his long sleeve white shirt was open. "Come on Walters, let's get out of here, these women suck!"

"What's the problem Jonah."

"There's no problem, Walters, it's just that these women are some worn and tired prostitutes." Grateful I decided not to go in I watched Jonah get himself together. By this time, I felt a bit hungry. "Hey, Jonah, let's go and get some Marine Corps chow, what do you say friend?"

"I agree a hundred percent, Walters." We both laughed thinking of how raucous Jonah had been in the States. He had changed over the months, hopefully for the better. I truly hoped he'd get over Monique; it appeared she did have him over a barrel. Maybe Jonah didn't have the influence Monique may have thought he had being that Jonah happened to be white. If she came from Upstate, she definitely knew what being influential was. Jonah was not dirt poor, but he wasn't the upper-class white; he did have to work for money. "Hey, Jonah, why'd you break out of there like that?"

"Walters, when a woman wants you to stay with her for another session, either she's lonely or money hungry. This one I just screwed was okay, but it's not like when I'm with Monique, I felt strange. And when she reached for me as I dressed, I high tailed it out of there!" As we crossed the street to go to chow, I couldn't help but feel a bit for my friend.

After spending the weekend with my friend Jonah, I awakened Monday morning to a screaming Sergeant Larsen. "Get out of the rack! Time for P.T.!" I scrambled as best I could to land on my feet. Larsen's assistants were in other cubicles screaming and yelling getting everyone ready to hit the road. It was not even 6:00 a.m. yet, so I had to force myself to get dressed. Outside the Barracks, the company C.O. was waiting. As all companies assembled, we then get under way. "Jumping

Jacks begin!" Everyone mechanically started doing the exercise. After about fifty, we began doing pushups. After five sets of ten, we paired off and did sit-ups. Grateful when we finished, we all fell in formation to double time. I dreaded this moment, but I knew that I had to do it. As companies divided into each separate one Sergeant Larsen begin singing cadence, "up in the morning in the rising sun, gonna run all day until the run is done. Urraah, good for me, good for you, gimme some P.T.!" As we echoed Larsen, the arduous task began.

When work wound down for the day, I couldn't help but think of Jonah. He said that he was in love with a black woman. Not that I carried any resentment toward them, but Jonah didn't strike me as a man who'd fall in love that quickly especially with a black girl. The rumors that floated around about black girls were that they loved sex, illicit or not. Of course one couldn't believe everything he heard, but a white man knew when to take the chance of loving a Negro. Sure, being that Jonah was a New Yorker, gave him the upper hand when it came to these matters, but it appeared that the love bug had stricken him. I hoped my friend could keep his composure. He certainly appeared to be rocked by the whole affair. And his girl notified him that she carried Jonah's child it didn't seem legitimate to me, but why was she toying with Jonah's feelings. Was it a scam to get money or did Monique truly love Jonah as he said. I couldn't put it all together, but I knew there were things that Jonah had not told me. Knowing Jonah there was something very important that Monique had learned of Jonah and now she held him hostage. Lieutenant Wikenburg wanted to talk to me this evening after work. Clearing my mind of Jonah's hassle, I readied myself for the meeting with Wikenburg.

"At ease lance corporal Walters, have a seat."

"Yes, sir!" I took the seat across from the Lieutenant.

"The reason I wanted to talk to you lance corporal is that we have a situation here."

"Yes sir?"

"Lance corporal, do you know that your dad is requesting that you be taken back to the States?"

"No, I know nothing of it sir." I said totally surprised. The Lieutenant sensing my discomfort stated reassuringly, "don't worry Walters, he only feels you'd be better off in America. You know he's lobbying to be a politician once he's discharged?"

"I've been hearing rumors of it from my grandmother sir, but just that rumors."

"I see; listen Walters, how would you like to become an Officer?" Wikenburg eyed me sternly. "Sir, I need a couple of months to see whether or not I'd be able to serve in the Corps for a year sir."

"I see. Well, I'm keeping my eye on you Walters, we don't want to upset the Colonel."

"Yes sir." The Lieutenant dismissed me. As I headed to the Barracks, I decided to skip chow and to call Jonah to clarify my ignorance. It took half an hour, but Jonah finally came to the phone.

"What's up Walters?"

"Hey, listen my friend you have me worried sick about you now, what's up with you and Monique?"

"I knew you'd figure it out sooner or later. You know you should become a lawyer."

"Well, Jonah?"

"Okay Walters; my aunt died several months ago and she left me a trust. Monique knew the family well and she heard about the trust."

"How much Jonah?"

"Over a half million."

"What!" I quickly calmed myself. Jonah, how could he not tell me this vital truth? Now it made sense. Monique wasn't going to leave Jonah she wanted control. Jonah sensed my uneasiness.

"Walters, I'm ashamed of it, but I didn't want you to think I was weak."

"Jonah, I've always knew you to be a straight shooter and a good Marine, I'd never put you down."

"Walters, I know Monique is trying to pin me down, but I do love her."

"Jonah, bring her to Okinawa and you'll find out what she wants she may actually love you."

"I'm hoping so Walters, I feel a great deal better that I did Saturday I mean I was really in the dumps." I had learned a great deal about him. He had met his match in Monique and I knew it.

We said our goodbyes. I decided to take a shower and then get something to eat at the snack bar before going out to meet Cameko. I didn't know what to expect, but I was ready for anything. Not traveling with anyone tonight, I wondered how everything would go. I quickly undressed and headed for the showers. Being that payday came that Friday; I knew that the crowd would be sparse at best. After showering I dressed and went to the Base snack bar. I ate four pieces of fried chicken. It helped but it wasn't quite as filling as good ole Marine Corps chow. While eating I pondered about the time I planned to spend with Cameko. 1930 hours, I still had a moment or two. I knew Cameko got off work in an hour or so, so I'd wait here a spell. I did not want to be caught in the streets by myself until I gained a bit of experience.

I hoped that Cameko had remembered and would be there waiting for me. Tucker had a previous engagement; he wanted to drink with some friends at the enlisted club. Drinking had its place, but I saw it as a danger to get addicted to king alcohol. So many people over the years have fell by the wayside. I'd respect Mr. Liquor now, and for the rest of my life to be perfectly honest. Bored, but after leaving the club, I finally hailed a cab. Hopefully this relationship with Cameko would blossom and I get some much-needed action.

I woke up at 1:30 a.m. the following morning. Cameko lay sprawled out naked next to me. She had a relatively nice physique. Her breast was rather small, but she had large nipples which I thoroughly enjoyed manipulating. Cameko remained silent during our lovemaking and she was very submissive. Tucker never schooled me about Cameko's lovemaking. I wondered did he really know. It could have possibly been my own assumptions, but it appeared that Cameko never really made love, she only let men thrash her for money. As horny as I had been, I still took my time. I had felt the explosion when I violently thrust into Cameko. Yes, she had been around the block and could receive my organ while I pumped with great force. The orgasm shook me, but I continued to love her. Cameko seemed to convulse a bit, but I dare not ask. I continued kissing her with deep French kissing until exhaustion got the better of me. I'd say five minutes later Cameko was fast asleep.

She had left her job with me as soon as I arrived. Surprised that she had decided to take me home I eagerly went with her. She even paid for the cab. Tucker, for all his bravado either liked bragging or he just didn't have the tools to pleasure the fair lady. I had to retake my assessment of Tucker. He appeared to have had a good thing with Cameko yet he apparently let it slip by. Cameko stirred and opened her eyes, she immediately went for my organ. A good sign if I estimated correctly. "Evdreeet," cameko did her best to pronounce my name. "You have to go back to base!"

"Yes, I know Cameko, I'll be fine, I'm almost ready to leave, just composing myself that's all."

"You like me Evdrett?"

"Just call me Walters, Cameko, and yes, I like you a lot."

"That makes me happy Walters, I wish you can come back when you want, just come after ten at night and when you come you can wait for me here."

"Are you going to give me a key?"

"Yes, I do, for you okay." I moved over and gave Cameko a kiss.

"Thanks sweet heart that's great!" I lie back down and wrapped Cameko in my arms. I could feel my erection coming again. Cameko felt it too, for she went flat on her back and opened her legs. As tempting as it was, I couldn't do it for being spent. "Listen Cameko, you have just given me more that I could handle. Why don't we lay here and hold each other until about 5:00 okay?"

"I'll set alarm for you Walters."

"Good, I appreciate that Cameko." We snuggled up to each other and relaxed. I started thinking of the things I needed to do to improve my current situation. I realized Okinawa to be an Island and there is so much one could do, but I wanted to explore life and walking just didn't sit well with what I wanted to do. Just before falling asleep I pictured an automobile.

The alarm startled me. "Damn! I'd better get moving." I thought to myself. Cameko still slept. I quickly dressed and left five twenties on Cameko's lamp stand. I quietly exited the apartment. It was small, but very well decorated. One could tell that Cameko had been there a while; I wondered how long she had been in the business. I remembered where I was so that I could locate the place my next visit. At night the place looked rather nice, but in the aftermath it appeared to be neat, but extremely modest to say the least.

Near Gate Two Street I easily hailed a cab. I knew what I was getting into right now wasn't the picture I had for myself as a kid, but I at least experienced what my curiosity led me too no matter how twisted things seemed to have become. Life as a Marine meant that I'd have to possibly fight in a war, and perhaps lose my life, yet I knew that when I joined the Military, so I prepared myself for it. The cab driver caught my attention. "Camp Kinser Honcho, quickly!"

"Okay, G.I. we go to Kinser."

CHAPTER FOUR
THE RIDE

Three months had passed since I had arrived on Okinawa. Two weeks ago, I purchased a 78 Datsun 280Z. The car, a very impressive vehicle, was lime green with no dents. The paint job, very shiny; the luster happened to be so great that I could see myself when I stood next to it. It ran great too. It purred like a kitten that just ate dinner. I paid over five thousand dollars for it. The Gunnery Sergeant who sold it to me had been on the Island for three years and had been transferred over to Guam. He didn't want to sell it, but he also didn't like the idea of lugging it around from Island to Island. I knew I had Gunny Robertson by the balls, and he knew it, but he had really given me good advice on how to survive Okinawa. The Gunny had happily married an Okinawan native some two years ago. So I purchased it from Gunny with no arguments and gladly paid the cash.

I had been seeing Cameko sparingly now. As it turned out she not only liked me, she liked several other Americans. Tucker, for all his bravado, didn't know a damn thing about Cameko. I had been spying on her without telling her I had wheels. She had no idea I watched her come in and out of the club with different men. She wouldn't take them home; she'd always go to different hotels. I still visited her, but I sort of drew away from her. By now I had begun to visit Whisper Alley regularly. I had been going to get a short time for at least two months. The sex was hard and raw, which I had begun to like. Now, Whisper Alley had proven that I had a hidden agenda with ladies of ill repute. Tucker had left the Island, so I traveled alone most of the time to the Alley. On one occasion I met a rather mature as well as attractive woman who called herself Mary. I knew it was a pseudo name, but I rather liked sticking to something simple like Mary. On a breezy Tuesday evening after running six miles around the Base, I decided to burn off some steam and go to Whisper Alley.

Mary had me giving her different items such as cigarettes, liquor, and female articles. It always tore at me to watch the cashiers at the PX stare at me purchasing the feminine products. I had to be careful, especially with the liquor and tobacco. A Marine could wind up in serious trouble if the ration was exceeded. Good money swarmed around the black market; sex too for that matter, so I always got a non-drinker to come with me to the package store and use his ration. Sometimes I'd give them a night on the town by riding through parts of the city.

When I arrived on Gate two, I quickly parked in a low-profile area behind the action so that I wouldn't be so visible. With my goods, I quickly rushed to Whisper Alley to Mary's small room. "Hello G.I. What you got for Mary tonight!"

"I have two bottles of Chivas Regal Mary."

"Toxon good, I make a lot of money with Poppasan."

"Good, now let's get down to business okay." Mary gave a perky smile,

"Short time G.I.?"

"Yeah, Mary, you give me five thousand yen and a short time and I'll call it even." Mary hesitated a minute, watching me in the process. "Okay, that's good, I do." With my erection fully charged, I quickly undressed. Mary did the same; we both stood there naked with Mary checking out my goods. "You nice size, I like." Mary said as she lies on her back on the mattress.

The room was dark and musty. I knew in the daylight this would be a dilapidated building at best. I gingerly got on top of Mary she expertly guided me into her warmth. I ejaculated quickly, within twenty seconds, convulsing for several seconds. Relieved, I stayed inside of Mary. "G.I. come again?" Mary asked encouraging me to keep going. Even though the sensation was so sensitive I could barely stand it, I kept gyrating on Mary. I began to thrust like an animal trying to unload again. After ten minutes of violent thrusting so hard that my thighs trembled, I climaxed again in Mary's steamy love tunnel. Breathing heavily, I felt my penis involuntarily jerking. "You stay inside of me G.I.!" I wondered if Mary got excited. I quickly dismissed the idea. There was no telling how many years Mary had spent here. Curious, I decided to ask Mary the inevitable question. "Mary, how long have you been here?"

"Too long G.I.!" Mary commented although not the least bit exasperated. She did appear to be breathing a bit out of the norm. I could not be positive, but it appeared that Mary liked the sensations of screwing. "Call me Walter, Mary, Okay?"

"Okay, I'll call you Walter." Mary never showed any signs of sadness, but appeared to accept her life as a sex tool. Mary, a decent enough looking woman; slim with good breast and no wrinkles. I assumed about thirty-five to forty. She had shoulder length hair, which coupled with her slender physique, left the door open for many visitors. "Do you want to talk about it?" I asked as I reached for my shorts. Mary, still naked pressed her warm body against me. "I like you Walter, maybe you come to my place okay."

"Why do you like me Mary is it short time?" I asked trying to bait her.

"You nice guy; quiet and smart. Very handsome."

"Thank you, Mary, and yes I'll go home with you." Mary released me and started dressing. "You dress now Walter, we go to my place." Silently I dressed. I wondered why Mary had taken such a liking to me. Not one to argue I remained silent. Mary disappeared into a little backspace and spoke to a male whom I didn't know was there. They spoke Okinawan which I didn't catch everything, but it sounded friendly enough. Mary soon reappeared. "Let's go Walter." We walked out of the small room into the breezy night. Okinawa, not a frigid place, but cool enough. I noticed out of the corner of my eye the stares from Americans and Okinawans, but I played it well not letting it phase me. I guided Mary to my car. When we got there, Mary was shocked. "You have car Walter?"

"Surprise Mary, yeah, I do. Do you like it?"

"Beautiful!" Mary semi screamed. I opened the door for Mary, who happily slipped into the vehicle. "This is nice Walter." I appreciated Mary's observance. I started the engine. "Where too Mary?"

"I live close by Walter. Go straight and turn on Third Street from Gate Two." I put the car in drive and eased my way in traffic, which was light at this hour. I checked the time, almost ten p.m. I still had an hour or so before I had to head back to Base.

It took at least ten minutes to get to Mary's house. Tucked away in a tightly kept residential area, I was surprisingly impressed. The neighborhood, with dozens of homes, appeared decent. Mary, I don't know where she got it, had more than a little bit of money. When we got to the front door, Mary took out a key and opened the door. A charming and well kept, small and neat home sat there for me to view. The white walls were immaculate. The sea blue divan was the only piece of furniture in the living room. The medium size television, which surprised me, sat opposite the couch. As I stood there admiring the scenery, Mary interrupted me, "Walter, you like?"

"Yes, Mary, very much. Why isn't your place more decorated?"

"I don't understand Walter."

"Do you want more stuff?" I tried to make my question plain so Mary would understand. "Oh, I like it this way it is easy to clean." Before we could comment any further two young girls entered the room. Both appeared to be teenagers, with one of them being at least seventeen. "These are my daughters Walter." I stood there stunned. These girls obviously had American blood in them. I motioned to introduce myself. "I'm Walters." The girls giggled and turned away. Mary spoke. "Walter, I tell my daughter's when I find nice G.I. I bring here to my home. So now they both know you nice guy. Yuriko is the oldest. "Yuriko, come here!" The bigger of the two girls timidly came forward. "Yuriko, this is Walter." Yuriko avoided eye contact, but managed to say "hi." I reached for her hand. "Hello Yuriko, I'm glad to meet you."

"Me too." Yuriko held out her hand and gently held mine. I held back knowing Mary watched intently. Mary spoke in Okinawan and Yuriko quickly left the room. Mary turned to me, ignoring the other girl, "listen, Walter, let's sit here on the sofa." We both sat down. "Walter, I bring you here because I did not want to talk in front of my boss; he very tough on me to make money. I had to give him one hundred dollars so I could leave."

"Really?"

"Yes, he say I lazy woman, I need to work." Mary giggled and stood. "Walter, I will get us a drink."

"Okay, Mary." I sat there and waited while Mary left the room. The picture on the wall was huge. It appeared to be a portrait of an influential Japanese man. As I studied the rest of the sitting room, I wondered why Mary took off her shoes, but did not ask me to the same. It did feel a bit awkward. Mary quickly came back with two plastic cups. "Here Walter, you take this."

"Thank you, Mary." We both then touched glasses.

"What is this, Mary?"

"It's American liquor, Seagram's."

"I see. Listen, Mary, why did you bring me here?"

"Walter, I want to ask you something."

"Yes, Mary."

"Do you come from nice home in the States? I mean do you…" Mary turned away. "Do you mean have money?"

"I mean do you have good heart Walter?"

"I care about people Mary if that's what you mean." Mary went on.

"The reason I ask Walter is that I have been to America before, San Diego."

"Really!"

"Yes, I spent four years with my first."

"Why did you come here again Mary?" Without flinching Mary said,

"He gave me two daughters and then he left me by myself for another girl, an American hakogen."

"What!"

"A white woman." I obviously knew that Mary's husband was white from the girls' color and features. "Mary, how did you get back here?"

"He gave me a hundred thousand dollars Walter, so when he left, I came back to Okinawa the next week. He wasn't nice man that's why I ask you."

"I see, I understand now." I put my arm around Mary who came closer.

"Walter, you know what's funny?"

"What's that Mary."

"I saw him on Whisper Alley and we had sex together." I looked at Mary incredulously.

"Are you serious Mary?"

"Yes, he is good lover Walter, like you." I blushed a bit before catching myself. "Thank you, Mary, I appreciate that." Mary laughed, a loud shrill that sort of sounded like relief more than anything else.

I watched Mary as she relaxed a bit. I could see now that she happened to be a very attractive woman. "So, Mary, if you mind my asking, why did you come to Whisper Alley?" Mary put her empty glass down. The liquor appeared to ease her inhibitions. "I stay at Whisper Alley because I like it. I knew that Okinawan people would shun me and my daughters because of them being half American." Surprised, I interrupted Mary. "I thought Okinawans loved Americans." Mary gave me a quizzical look. "Walter, do you really believe that?"

"Well, yes, I do Mary." Mary seemed to sober up a bit before commenting, "Walter, you remember Hiroshima?" That question hit me like a bombshell. I had completely forgot about other people's feelings. I was so wrapped up in my fantasies that I had completely forgotten about the world political struggles. From Mary's reminders I realized that for the most part that Okinawans tolerated the United States presence because they had to at this point.

"I did not mean to upset you Walter, but it is only the truth."

"I understand Mary." My spirits were dashed and I could feel my penis shrinking. Even after two orgasms, I could feel the blood flowing. Mary revived my spirits. "You see the picture, Walter?"

"Yes Mary, I do."

"That's my grandfather, General Takosuge. He was in the Japanese Army."

"I see, did you ever meet him in person?"

"Yes, when I was a little girl, I watched my mother paint the picture on the wall." Impressed, nonetheless I remained silent. Mary went on. "Walter, don't worry I like you okay."

"That's nice Mary, I am still a bit embarrassed I had completely forgotten about America's atrocities against the Japanese. Hopefully I won't forget again. Now about your grandfather, did he like Americans?"

"Oh, no, grandfather hated Aryans. He thought that they were double-tongued traitors. The old Japanese custom didn't allow Japanese women to intermingle with Americans. Things have changed Walter." I could have set there and listened to Mary for hours. Even though she had a bit of a broken dialect, she spoke English well. "You know Mary we completely got off the subject you never told me why you are on Whisper Alley."

"I like the money and sex Walter." Taken aback a bit, I didn't think Mary would be so forward. She surprised me. "So I take that as a good thing."

"Yes, Walter, it is. I do plan to stop if I can find a good man." A little uneasy at Mary's revelation, still I pressed forward. "A good man huh, well you'll find one."

"I think already I find him." Mary gave me the eye. I looked squarely back at her. "Mary, do you bring men here a lot?"

"No, just special people I trust. You are the first G.I." Mary touched my thigh. "You are very nice man Walter, I like your company."

"So you really mean what you said about me being good in bed Mary?"

"American woman never tell you that!"

"Mary, I'm an inexperienced man with the ladies. Usually I only dated them." Mary quizzically looked at me before smiling. "You know Walter I never knew you to be a virgin." Mary giggled again, a girlish laugh, I could see her good nature. "Walter, I bring you here because…" Mary grew silent. I could tell that she was fighting her words. "Listen Walter, I like you and I like when you bring me things from Base." Mary again looked right at me waiting for a response. I said nothing. Mary, noticing my reluctance continued. "Walter, you bring me things and I could sell them. I tell you what to bring okay?" I felt as though I was in a dream and wouldn't wake up, I knew that this act would be dangerous, but I was in this thing up to my neck.

"Mary, I could get in a lot of trouble you know!"

"No, you listen to me and you be okay."

"Have you done this before Mary?" Mary didn't hesitate.

"Yes, with my ex-husband. We make a lotta money Walter."

"I see. Did you run into any problems Mary?"

"No, we sell everything, not just cigarettes and liquor."

"What do you want me to do Mary?" Mary put her arms around me and stated, "Marry me!" Taken aback, but a bit pleased I asked, "What's init for me Mary?"

"Anything here, you want you take!"

"Anything?"

"Yes." I could tell Mary knew what was on my mind. Yuriko was of age and she happened to be very desirable. "We'll talk about it tomorrow, Mary."

"Walter, do you want to or no say now!"

"I want to Mary, but give me some time alright."

"I give you one-week okay Walter?"

"That's fine. You know, Mary, I best be heading back to Base, it's getting late. I'll see you Friday and we'll talk."

"Come to Whisper Alley, I'll be there okay."

"That's fine." We both stood and I gave Mary a peck on the cheek before departing the small but exclusive home.

I could say Mary did well for herself. She appeared to have more to offer than Cameko. Cameko seemed to be genuine, but she was a petty hustler. Mary on the other hand wanted the big time. I contemplated going over to Cameko's place, but instinct pushed me away from it. Okinawa was a small place and Gate Two and the Alley were no exceptions I could just about count on Mary knowing Cameko. I didn't want any confrontations not now anyway.

I quickly drove back to Base. It was well past one in the morning and I knew to get some rest would suit its purpose. I could push myself to get through the workday. As I lay in the rack, I thought of everything that Mary and I discussed. I knew that Mary was not a young girl, but she had sex appeal to her. I wasn't too keen on marriage, but I the wolf that I had turned into felt my loins at the thought of Yuriko. She had a grown-up physique and a young girl's mind, which excited me most exquisite.

When I climbed into my bunk, I could sense the murmurings of the other Marines. I realized that word was out about my dealings with the natives. Most Marines in our unit either abstained or only went to town to relieve tension. I, On the other hand, relished my current situation. Sure, having a vehicle gave me a distinct advantage, but I still carried the title Marine and we happened to be a Band of Brothers. Tucker no doubt spread some pretty juicy gossip about me concerning Cameko. And in Tucker's viewpoint Cameko was one hot babe. Yes, she being an attractive woman accelerated the flame, so I knew better than to gloat. Regardless of the beauty of women it took money ninety percent of the time, so there was no need for bad blood. Tucker may have just tried to make me look good being that I was a newbie to the Islands, yet discretion was the key here on the Rock. I floated into a troubled sleep dreaming of Yuriko.

The next day at work my assumptions about negative vibes were correct. Curtis, who had earned his Corporal, stripes back and now he was Sergeant Larsen's assistant. During formation Curtis was eyeing me more than normal. I knew something was up. Curtis dismissed the group and called me, "Lance corporal Walters could I see you for a moment?"

"Sure Corporal Curtis what's up."

"Lance corporal Walters, word is that you are staying up at some pretty late hours. You are going to have to tighten up."

"I'm okay Corporal, I'm just getting my wings under me."

"Word to the wise Walters, drinking and lack of sleep are the things that a Marine can do without you get the point!"

"I do Corporal."

"Remember what I told you when you first came to the Rock? Don't lose yourself."

"I'll remember that Corporal and besides, I'm not drinking much at all."

"It's your life Walters." With that Corporal Curtis walked away. I tried to reason with myself. Okinawa sure made Individuals sensitive. I wonder was it sex or my car. I knew most Marines were on a tight budget and by now most knew my dad was an officer in the Army. At first, I didn't give these things much thought, but now they bounced around in my mind. Moments later I was called into the office. I had a run to Camp Hansen to pick up supplies for the Supply unit. It would be an all-day job. I got my trip chart and headed out to vehicle 075. This happened to be a pretty good running troop carrier. As I prepared to go on the trip, Private Lonny Dunbar, a newbie, jumped into the cab. "I was ordered to go with you Walters!"

"Hop in rookie."

"Thanks." Dunbar nimbly jumped into the cab. A short and stocky Marine, Dunbar didn't get out of the shop much. A bit timid with the trucks, Dunbar who personally had asked 2nd Lieutenant Wikenburg for permission not to drive, and Wikenburg had been known for respectfully honoring his troops request didn't push Dunbar, but let him have a little time to gather himself while he adjusted to life on the Rock. I playfully asked Dunbar if he wanted to drive. "Are you serious Walters?"

"No, I'm only kidding Private. But tell me something Dunbar, what's your plan in the Corps?"

"I don't know yet. Do my three years and see, maybe join the Air Force or something."

"Why the Air Force?" I asked a bit curious.

"Well, I want to be Air Force Security and I thought with Marine discipline I'd have enough training to carry me through a twenty-year stint."

"I see. Why not do a career as a Jarhead Dunbar?"

"Politics Walters. You see being a Marine is serious business. You never know how your mind will turn you know what I mean. I knew of a fellow who did a career in the Corps, and just like that after twenty years the guy blew his brains out."

"Is that so!" I exclaimed pondering a bit on what Dunbar had just said. He appeared to have a game plan in spite of himself. "Listen, Dunbar, you appear to have thought things well."

"Yeah, coming from Iowa let me tell you there's always plenty of room for thinking." Dunbar then turned his attention to me. "So Walters, word around Barracks is that you're a regular stud."

"Well, Dunbar, don't let scuttlebutt determine what you think about me alright!" I started easing away from the Motor Pool lot. "Sure Walters, anyway I think it's great that a guy can get laid and such. Lord knows I won't touch a Jap though."

"Why not Dunbar?"

"Hey, listen, didn't you hear about what they did in Nam?"

"No, please inform me."

"Well, when American Soldiers would rape the villagers, they'd put razor blades wrapped up in small balls and stuff them in their vaginas. And then on the down stroke the ole penis would split in two!" I flinched at the thought.

"Where on earth did you hear that Dunbar!"

"Word gets around Walters. Anyway, where are you from?"

"I'm from Nebraska."

"A Cornhusker huh."

"Yes, I really miss being called that."

"I bet." Dunbar quipped. I settled in on the main road. Dunbar appeared to be fascinated with the civilized way the Okinawans lived. "I thought Japanese to be primitive people still living in straw huts."

"No, and I don't think they put razor blades up the vagina either."

"How do you know Walters?"

"I've been with a few and let me tell you, I'm still functional. It's pleasurable too. "I could see Dunbar getting curious. "Well, Walters, do you spend a lot of money on women?"

"I've spent my share, but that's anywhere you go Dunbar, women and money are inseparable."

"I agree, but you know Walters, I'm going to save money to buy a home someday. I can't let it go on whores."

"Smart choice Dunbar, maybe you'll get a nice home, who knows."

"What about you Walters, you want a home?"

"I already have one. My grandmother promised me hers."

"Good deal, so now what screw all the whores and then go back stateside?"

"Correction my friend. Find a nice one and then go back Stateside."

"If it's possible Walters." Dunbar then gave me a quizzical look. I saw him out of the corner of my eye. "Listen, Dunbar, it's not only possible it's very attainable for me."

"I don't get you Walters, how can you find a nice whore?"

"Well, I said getting a bit exasperated at the young fellow. "I'm not trying to find a nice whore, but if I do, sure, I'll take her home." Dunbar, it seemed, perceived me to be a bit twisted. "Walters, what would your parents think?" I admit Dunbar had me cornered with that question I squirmed a bit before answering him. "Look, Dunbar, at this point in my life I can't be concerned with what others think. This is my life and I'm prepared to give my life in my country's defense, what the hell do my parents have to do with it!" Dunbar didn't answer but looked longingly at the scenery while I drove on the main road. I drove the 5-ton defensively knowing the military vehicle stuck out like a sore thumb. Noticing Dunbar's silence I continued. "Dunbar do you figure to be on the Rock a whole year without sex?" Dunbar became unraveled.

"You know Walters, I didn't figure on that, what do you think?"

"Dunbar you might consider going to Naha, the girls are not whores and you might just meet someone."

"I'm not against whores Walters, I just don't like losing a lot of money and then leaving the Island broke."

"I see your point Dunbar. I think you should go with your gut feeling."

"Really Walters."

"Yes, Dunbar, go with your gut." Dunbar relaxed a bit before adding, "You know Walters I wanted to talk with this W.M. whom I met at the club the other night."

"That's great Dunbar, you have an opportunity to really benefit from Okinawa, a female Marine! Boy that's really unusual."

"Walters, she's not the prettiest girl, but…"

"Dunbar, when the lights are out and you're both naked skin to skin looks means very little my friend."

"I agree Walters, good point." I then came up on a stoplight; I geared down and waited for the light to change. Dunbar appeared to really appreciate my advice. Not a handsome fellow himself, Dunbar should have been grateful for an American to even notice him. As the light turned green, I began the routine of shifting gears in the cargo/troop carrier. Dunbar seemed to like riding in the vehicle, hopefully he'd get over his fear and begin driving himself. Traveling south I saw the expressway exit. I wheeled the lumbering machine toward the expressway. I was hoping to catch up with Jonah. I hadn't heard from him in a while and I wondered what had transpired between he and Monique. I thrust the beast in fifth gear as I mashed the pedal to the floor.

CHAPTER FIVE
SURPRISE

    I could barely wait for Friday to come around. Meeting Jonah Tuesday on my run to Camp Hansen helped me to catch up on my friend's status. Jonah had extended on the Island for three years so that he and Monique could get married and live on the Rock. Surprisingly, Monique agreed to come to Okinawa. In Jonah's words, Monique wanted to get away from the Big Apple anyway and to live in the Orient was a unique opportunity. Monique the academian, wanted to study various languages while she attempted to teach. She had her teaching credentials, which in my opinion had flattered Jonah so much that he never let up. I admired Jonah's integrity.

    He had to spend a year at Camp Hansen and then he'd be able to transfer to Camp Foster. Jonah had mentioned he'd be a dispatcher in the near future. Monique had been on the Island less than 30 days and she already had an automobile. Monique already landed a job working at the Base P.X. on Camp Foster. She didn't want to get out of sync, so she continued to work until she had the baby. After informing me on the latest, Jonah had to hurry back to his duty station. I said farewell to my good friend.

It was well after 3 p.m. before my truck was loaded. I could sense that Jonah had overwhelmed Dunbar. Not only a fast talker, but also Jonah spoke of things few Marines accomplished. Having an educated woman willing to come to the Rock with her man, which impressed the observant but intimidated Dunbar. I rather liked to see the reaction from Dunbar, it may have shown him that my level of living wasn't just whore chasing, but a calculated man who thrived for the good life.

On the way back to Camp Kinser I questioned Dunbar, who remained silent while I drove. "Listen Dunbar, what did you think of Jonah?"

"To be honest Walters, I didn't know what to think. The guy appears to be a very efficient Marine capable of controlling the ladies."

"Controlling the ladies?" I asked, quite shocked at the blunt statement.

"What I'm saying Walters is that your buddy convinced a woman to leave the States for Okinawa. That's influence if I ever seen it!"

"Well, Dunbar, you could do the same couldn't you?"

'Do you think I'd bring someone I loved over here to let her run wild on me with God know who? No way!"

"Dunbar, if you loved a woman and she loved you no matter where you lived it shouldn't make a difference." Even though I hated to admit it, Dunbar had made a valid point.

Although many Marines successfully married their sweethearts, the horror stories floated through the air. One in particular was of a Marine who loved his wife very much. After the Marine went on an Exercise with his unit, his dutiful wife begins to party. And before you knew it the wife was partying and screwing two to three men a week. There was even talk of Oriental men screwing her. It never materialized but money popped up as being the main reason for the infidelity. The poor Marine, his emotions getting the better of him, when he came off the exercise, stomped his wife until she was unconscious. He had fractured her skull and broke an arm and several ribs. The Marine who snitched on the wife turned out to be a spurned lover who couldn't accept rejection. The poor bastard received twenty years in Leavenworth. I got a grip on myself. Tragedy or not a man should not let the fear of infidelity keep him from love. I had to reason with Dunbar as I drove. "Dunbar, my friend, you must learn to love. Grow with your lover. Those poor saps that lost their mates probably got comfortable in the bottle and stopped caring. Any woman responds to continual love Dunbar." Silent for a minute Dunbar let everything soak in before stating, "It may not have been the bottle Walters, it could have been the old adage, once you catch the prey you stop hunting."

"Good point my friend, that may well be the answer." I had to respect Dunbar's wisdom. He didn't appear to be very wise, but someone had schooled him well.

As the truck lumbered down the road, we both fell silent letting the lesson we taught each other about love and women set in. Halfway through the expressway I listened to the familiar hum of the turbo as it whined melodiously with the engine. Dunbar appeared to be exhausted. We had been on our feet most of the day. Poor sap didn't expect his day to be so challenging. Before I knew it Dunbar was fast asleep. I made a mental note of it, so I'd drive carefully; I didn't want to injure the kid.

When we arrived on Camp Kinser, I noticed the time. It was after 1700 hours. I took the truck over to supply, who had been waiting for me. I quickly backed the truck into the warehouse. The Supply Marines quickly unloaded the truck with forklifts. Dunbar had gotten out of the truck and headed to the Barracks. After the truck was unloaded, I headed back to the Motor Pool. Corporal Curtis was there waiting for me. "What do you say Walters?"

"I'm fine Corporal,"

"Good. Everything go okay Walters?"

"The supplies are delivered and the truck is secured Corporal."

"Well done Walters. Finish up your trip ticket and you'll be done for the day."

"Aye aye, Corporal." I quickly finished up the ticket and turned it in to Corporal Curtis then I headed to the Barracks. After I arrived at the

Barracks I quickly showered and decided to go to the Enlisted Club. I dressed casual for the occasion and headed out. I decided to drive my car over so drinking tonight had to be kept at a minimum.

The Country and Western music blared as I entered the Club. It appeared to be a popular night as it was very crowded, standing room only. I grabbed a spot and hugged the wall with my back. The Marines were frantically trying to get to the females who loved every minute of the attention they were getting. Through all the smoke I saw Dunbar and his girl dancing. He had gotten here quick that's for sure. The woman he danced with didn't look so bad from my angle. I wondered why Dunbar complained earlier. As I eyed Dunbar, a rather cute girl came up to me. "Excuse me, would you mind buying me a drink?"

"Sure, young lady, but would you rather we go out in town and buy it it's much more exciting."

"I'd never step out to that cesspool!"

"You mean Gate Two Street?"

"Yes!" She seemed to be getting a bit perturbed.

"Well young lady, I mean Naha, it's on the opposite end of the Island. It's a regular city."

"Oh really." She seemed to be interested again. "I'm Madison."

"I'm Everett, nice to meet you."

"So Everett, how are we going to get there?"

"I have a car."

"Oh, I still want that drink." I quickly called for a waitress who happened to be waiting a table near us. Madison quickly spoke up, "An Ice Tea please." The waitress took the order and quickly disappeared in the crowd. Surprisingly Madison slipped her arm around mine. She whispered in my ear, "You know it is pretty noisy in here."

"Yes, I noticed." I put my arm around Madison's waist, she didn't protest, but snuggled closer to me. "You know Everett, you seem familiar, where are you from in the States?"

"Nebraska."

"Oh really, you know that's interesting. I sort of recognized you, but I can't be sure where from in Nebraska?" I hesitated a bit before answering. I saw something being pieced together by Madison who appeared to be more interested than meeting me. "Lincoln, Madison, Lincoln, Nebraska."

"Well, guess what Everett, I thought so, I'm from Lincoln too." Madison gave me a bear hug and gleefully shouted, "It's nice to meet someone from home."

"I feel the same way, Madison." I said taking in some ugly stares in the process. The waitress quickly dropped off the drink. "Two Dollars sir!" I quickly went into my pocket and fished out a five, "Keep the change okay."

"Why thank you sir." The waitress, a short and slender Okinawan put the money on her tray and quickly disappeared in the crowd. Madison took several gulps of the drink and then found a table to put the empty glass down on. "Let's go Everett!" Madison appeared to be very calculated, but it was interesting to say the least, so I followed her out of the E-club. "Boy, that music is certainly loud enough don't you think Everett?"

"Yeah, I could barely hear you talk Madison."

"It's much better out here. So where's your car Everett?"

"It's right over here Madison." I led her to my car.

Out in the bright light I could see Madison close up. A bit pudgy but not bad, short brunette hair, Madison stood at least six feet, a tall girl to say so myself. A bit awkward, Madison appeared to be growing into womanhood. "How old are you, Madison?"

"I'm seventeen, I'm just out of high school Everett."

"What's your last name Madison?"

"It's Bilkens Everett."

"Do you have a brother named Marshall Bilkens?"

"Yes, as a matter of fact, we went to the same High School."

"North East?" I asked my memory jarred in the process.

"Yes, how did you know?"

"He happened to be a school mate." Suddenly I pictured this gangly little girl always following her older brother around. She always got under Marshall's skin, but he looked out for his sibling. I looked over at Madison before opening the door. Very cute, even though she was a bit chubby, close up in the light she had an attractive face. "Here let me open that for you Madison."

"Thank you, Everett." Madison said and slipped in the front seat. "You know Everett, Marshall never forgot about you even after we moved from Lincoln." I nodded my head. Now it was coming to me; Marshall Bilkens had been a friend of mine since we enrolled as freshmen at North East. In the middle of his senior year Marshall had moved. I remembered his little sister, who now stood before me. "So, what made you join the Corps Madison?"

"Adventure Everett. I grew tired of corn and cattle, I wanted to see more of life that the State of Nebraska."

"Same here Madison. Sure, Nebraska is a nice peaceful place, but I agree one hundred percent."

"So, you're going to show me Naha huh?"

"Sure, Madison. By the way what makes you say Gate Two is a cesspool?"

"Because I hear all of the girls at the Barracks say so Everett." Madison gave me a funny look as if to say 'have you been there Everett?' I ignored her.

"You know, Madison, I've heard talk too, and there is a lot of lonely Marines over here on Okinawa, I'm surprised there aren't more places like Gate Two." Madison ignored me this time. She relaxed a bit as I eased out of the parking lot. "Nice car Everett, I bet you've spent a lot of money on it." Madison eyed me as I drove.

"Yes, I did young lady."

"For who Everett?" Madison tried pushing it out of me. I didn't respond, but I kept driving. Madison went on. "Anyway Everett it doesn't matter, I don't hold it against you. It's none of my business. I'm here for one year and then I'm going somewhere while I serve my country."

"So, are you saying that anything goes while you're here on the Rock?"

"Let's just say no strings, Everett." I soaked in Madison's statement. She obviously presented herself to me, but could I handle it? I knew a woman feeding off emotions couldn't screw without feelings. Madison appeared young and inexperienced. And from my visit with Cameko and Mary, I had become a pretty savvy lover. I could probably bring out Madison's heart, but could I handle all that now lay on my plate?

As we neared Naha, I could see Madison taking the sights in. Star struck was a better word. Myself, I felt like this was a whole world compared to Gate Two, nice, clean, and all lit up. The place, albeit size, resembled any typical city except for the Oriental style writing.

After five or so minutes of silence I spoke. "Listen, Madison, I know that being a long way from home you probably feel that what mommy and daddy don't know won't hurt them."

"No actually Everett, I kind of liked you from Nebraska, I wondered what happened to you. Marshall went off to school in Illinois. He's earning his Bachelors you know."

"So Madison, you've liked me since high school and now that Marshall's not around you still have that school girl crush?"

"No. Has anyone ever told you that you are incredibly handsome Everett?" Taken aback I smiled before answering, "Not the way you said it, Madison."

"You know Everett, I knew you before I came up to you, did you know me?"

"To be honest Madison, no I didn't. I thought you wanted company."

"So you thought I was a whore!" Madison said laughing, poking me in the ribs in the process. "No, not anything like that, it's just that I…" I had to admit Madison was right. I didn't answer, but I went down a side street and came upon several Bars. I parked next to the most colorful one and shut off the ignition. "Let's go inside and check it out Madison, okay?"

"Sure, I'll go inside, but Everett keep an eye on me, I'm a bit afraid."

"Why Madison?" I asked genuinely perplexed.

"White slavery silly. Remember the prostitution ring that's exploited around the world?"

"If you're not sure you want to go in, we can go somewhere else, don't put yourself through this Madison."

"No Everett this is fine." We both got out of the Datson and went inside the club. Two or maybe three people were inside drinking. Good, I held Madison by the hand and led her to a seat. The patrons appeared to be preoccupied to notice us. The Club smelled murky, like cigarettes and of all things human bodies. A bit of alcohol scent filled the air. The lights were low and the place looked like a low budget joint sort of like someone made a home into a bar. It would suit us just fine. I sat next to Madison; I had completely overlooked how Eastern men viewed Caucasian women. Now I not only had the dilemma of juggling women, but Madison's safety as well.

We ordered segrams seven and soda. Fortunately, the waitress understood us. As we sipped on our drinks, Madison looked me in the eyes and stated solemnly, "You know Everett, I miss home."

"How long have you been on the Rock Madison?"

"A little over two months I guess, I'm going through a transitional period."

"What's your M.O.S.?"

"Oh, I'm in administration, what about you Everett?"

"I'm a vehicle operator."

"A truck driver!" Madison squealed. Laughing at her tone I had to reassure Madison that truck driving is what I wanted to do in the Corps. "Gee Everett of all things a truck driver!"

"Yes, and I'm perfectly happy doing it Miss Bilkens."

"Sure, anyway Everett I meant what I said about no strings."

"Madison, a relationship is based on emotions. Anytime bonding takes place emotions are sure to follow."

"But that's just it Everett, I know you and if I do get attached we do have some history and I feel better about it that way."

"I see. Well young lady I never much thought of you as someone I'd be romantically linked to."

"Speak for yourself Romeo because I've always liked you. I'd dream of you and I running off somewhere to a romantic bliss and here we are." Madison squirmed in her seat. I took that as a positive. I had never known Madison to display her sexuality. "Look Madison, I don't want to do anything we'll regret." Madison didn't flinch, but unbuttoned the top part of her blouse and put her hand on mine. "Everett, I've been on the Marines for eight months and I haven't had a man yet." Madison appeared to be affected by the drinks, or maybe like she said she is in the mood. I wanted to resist, but now my desire got involved. "I know you're a decent girl Madison and you are very desirable. If I get my hands on you sweet heart you will never be the same."

"Let's go Everett." With that Madison drank her drink and then she took mine and gulped it down. We quickly left the cozy club. My car seemed like a welcome relief. The club, although small had the Oriental flare. The music and everything spoke purely to the natives. I didn't understand the whining monologue or the style of music, but with the mood as it were, who cared.

I went further into Naha and located a fairly decent Hotel. "Is this okay Madison?"

"Sure, Tiger." Madison reached for my crotch and squeezed. She giggled at my erection. "Someone's horny."

"Yes, Madison, I am. You seem to be pretty heated up yourself." Madison quickly jumped out of the car. I did the same. The Hotel stood out among the other buildings. I had to admire the Okinawans they had good architectural designs constructed.

I held Madison's hand as we walked toward the Hotel entrance. When we got to the front desk, a polite and elderly gentleman greeted us. "May I help you?" He said it in pretty good English. "Yes sir, we'd like a room with a single bed."

"Yes, I will be glad to help you." The clerk then handed us a key. "That will be 50,000 yen or $200.00 in American money." I swallowed hard and I dug into my pockets. I had almost three hundred cash, which turned out to be a blessing. I handed the clerk the money and took the key from him. The clerk gave us a knowing smile, "Have a nice time sir."

"Thank you." Madison said not to be left out. As we marched up the stairs, which Madison insisted after much grabbing and petting we finally got to room 311.

Once in the room Madison grabbed me and held me in a lip block. I gave my tongue back to her. Madison took a step back and started unbuttoning her clothes. Dressed nice in a pink long sleeve shirt and white slacks, Madison was dressed for the occasion. I had jeans and a white polo shirt and I quickly stepped out of it. We both stood looking at each other in our underwear. I had to admit that Madison looked surprisingly good despite my reluctance to sleep with her. But when Madison slipped out of the pink bikini panties, which hugged her ample hips well all my resistance flew out of the third story window. With a fierce erection, I jumped out of my shorts and into a waiting Madison on the fluffy bed. When I touched the soft flesh of Madison, I knew this would be a memorable night. Madison let out a slight moan as I mounted her quivering and willing flesh and probed for paradise.

CHAPTER SIX
FIELD DAY

    I knew I was in way too deep. I still wanted Mary and Yuriko, but part of me desired Madison now that we had slept together. Madison still had a lot of the little girl in her. She spoke like an experienced woman, but I assumed that she had sex sparingly if at all. I really had to take my time with her. After our lovemaking session we spoke at length about Nebraska. Come to find out, we didn't live too far away from each other in Lincoln. After we had made love and left the Hotel room in Naha, I drove Madison back to Base. When I dropped Madison off at the W.M. Barracks, neither one of us wanted to talk. From Madison's story, she worshipped secretly in Lincoln, and she showed me a diadem. I instantly thought "Satan." It didn't upset me, it only presented a challenge. A relationship with a witch, surprisingly, I thought I could break Madison away from that cult, if that indeed was what it turned out to be. For right now I'd let it go just get to know her here on the Rock and then respond.

After a good night kiss Madison whispered in my ears, "You're my love slave Everett!" then she licked my ear lobe tickling me in the process. I liked my friend and I let her know it. "Madison, dear, I want you to stay here at the Barracks until I come for you. I mean it girl!" I hugged Madison and hugged her tight. "Madison this is the Rock not Nebraska. You have people from all over America here listen to me I know." Madison seemed to break, "Alright Everett I'll wait until you come and see me."

"So we have a plan?"

"Yes!" Madison reluctantly replied, she kissed me again before she got out of the car and walked up the stairs leading to the Barracks. I cruised out of the parking lot. All eyes were on me, which would begin my days as a player around the Base. I looked at my watch 2330 hours. I'd best get back to my bunk. I wanted to be thoroughly prepared for field day Thursday evening.

On the way to my Barracks I thought of the situation. Madison appeared to be a space case, pretty, but a bit off balance. Good enough for Uncle Sam, which meant she'd follow orders and hopefully they would be coming from me. I met Dunbar heading up the stairs to the Barracks. There were three or four Marines badgering him. Dunbar appeared to be to mashed up off booze to notice anything out of the ordinary. "Hey Dunbar, who's the dog you lead out of the E-Club?"

"None of your business Private Thorn!"

"Yeah, well I'll make it my business." Poor Dunbar was going to try and defend himself. This Thorn fellow looked mean. A tall rangy Marine with well-toned arms, he had a broad back and slim shoulders. Dangerous indeed. The other three Marines stayed in the shadows. Evidently to inebriated to be effective. As Dunbar reached for the stairs, Thorn grabbed him and yanked him away from the stairs. "Come on Dunbar, bastard, I'll kick your fucking ass!" Not to be out done Dunbar ripped free from the lanky Thorn. He appeared to be over six feet. He didn't look like our company so I asked him, "Where you from Marine?"

"Fuck you!"

"I wouldn't give you the chance. Marine now tell me what's this all about!" Thorn's being drunk helped him to pick up on my voice of authority. Thorn began to back off Dunbar, who stood crouched ready to pounce. "Listen," Thorn said, "This Bastard took my girl!"

"He did?"

"Yeah, he stole her from me. I was dancing with her at the Club and this jerk broke in."

"When did you first meet her Thorn?"

"Tonight, at the Club!"

"Well, you know what, she and Dunbar are going steady and for longer than tonight. You know Thorn I think everything is a big misunderstanding. Why don't you Marines sleep this off and then let the woman decide who she wants when everyone's sober." Thorn, though drunk, hesitated, but didn't dispute with me. He began walking away. The other Marines walked away behind him. When they were out of earshot, I looked at Dunbar. "What the hell was that all about!"

"Hell, Walters, I don't know; all I remember is that while I slow danced with my girl, this lean asshole started yelling saying that she was his girl. Of course I denied him and that's when the trouble started. As we were leaving the Club these four followed us. And when I left the W.M. Barracks, Thorn followed me here." I understood Dunbar's dilemma. Size played a key role in mingling with the ladies. It was the American way. Dunbar as muscular as he happened to be still didn't match up to taller and heavier Marines. It reminded me of the animal food chain. "Well, Dunbar, I don't think you've seen the last of Mr. Thorn!"

"I'll say. You know Walters, it would not be a bad idea to try Japanese girls after all. At least there's privacy."

"That's not the point Dunbar, the point is respect. And from the looks of things tonight even a Japanese girl might create tension. Understand?" Not realizing it, I had flexed my leadership skill. Now while promotion had not yet been mentioned I had heard that I'd be promoted to Corporal shortly. But for now, I had to pick up Dunbar's emotions. "Dunbar, you're a Marine and you need to start behaving like one!"

"What are you saying Walters?"

"The drinking, Dunbar, you have to cool it. You were practically beaten tonight and you could have lost your life!" Someone had to teach this kid that the game we play is for keeps and one false move could ruin a life in or out of the Military.

I led the drunken Dunbar upstairs and to his rack. I understood that Dunbar's condition needed to be addressed. For now, sleep was being the only remedy. After seeing Dunbar feebly crawl into his bunk, I went to mine. When I finally hit the rack, it was 2430 hours. Restless, I had a terrible time getting to sleep. And when I did, it felt like seconds had passed before reveille had been sounded. It felt like someone had hooked sandbags to my eyes as I tried to pull out of bed. Corporal Curtis kneeled over me as I tried to get up. "Get out of the rack Walters! He said as softly as a Marine Corporal could muster. I struggled, but I managed to get to my feet. "Rough night huh Marine?"

"No, actually Corporal I had the time of my life."

"Really." Curtis sneered; he no doubt thought I was with whores.

"Yes, Corporal Curtis I did. As a matter of fact, I plan to do it again someday." Curtis chuckled and went on to the next bunk. I quickly headed to the showers and prepared for the day.

The duty station had maintenance today. I knew that after work, field day was coming, but today at work, I had the privilege of sweeping the shop floor. We had an inspector coming today at 1200 hours, so everything had to be Marine Corps squared away. Word had it that Battalion Commander had taken a stroll through the shop and had gotten pissed at what he saw. So he ordered Lieutenant Wikenburg to get things satisfactory real quick. While I swept everything in file, Lance Corporal Maurice Filson came over. Filson, a Marine from Miami had been on the Rock for two years. He spoke a bit of Okinawan so he got around. "What do you say Walters?"

"I'm good Filson, what's up?"

"Well just thought I'd check on the player of the Orient. Oh, yeah, Walters I've been watching you and you are a smooth operator." I knew Filson to be a Marine that had contacts outside of the Corps. Rumor was that he affiliated with the Mob in the States. Normally, I didn't speak too much with Filson, so I was a bit surprised at the greeting, but I played the game anyway. "What makes you say that, Filson." Filson chuckled, looked away before saying, "with those wheels why not man you're a shoo in."

"Is that all that's on your mind Filson." I could sense as much.

"Well no Walters, but what I do have on my mind is making a bit of money and with a car like that! You game?"

"It depends Filson, there are thousands of ways to get in trouble over here on the Rock."

"Hey buddy, I wouldn't put you in jeopardy, you'll just transport some items for me solid?"

"I'd really have to look into it Filson maybe tonight at field day at the Barracks."

"Good enough Walters, good enough." Filson slipped smoothly away from me. I wondered what it was that he had in mind. Transporting alcohol and booze was one thing, but… I pushed the thought out of my mind and continued to sweep. After about two hours of constant sweeping formation was called by sergeant Larson. "Motor Pool, fall in!" All thirty or so Motor T Marines fell in formation. Larsen smiled as he yelled, "now good ole Lieutenant Wikenburg guaranteed me if Barracks pass inspection tomorrow, Marines we get Friday off!" The Motor Pool erupted in loud vicious war cries. Larsen let it go on for a while then reminded us that today is payday. After we received our checks, everything was secured and we were to begin field day. It wasn't 1500 hours yet, so I decided after we marched to the Barracks, I'd check on Madison.

Corporal Curtis did the honor of drilling us. His deep baritone voice easily held our attention as we marched to the beat of his cadence. When we arrived at the Barracks, all the troops agreed that we would start field day at 1800 hours so that everyone could eat chow. This suited me just fine, as it would give me an opportunity to search for my turtle dove. I had been thinking about Madison all day. I knew she worked at H&S Headquarters', so I headed up that way. I figured I'd spend as much time as allowed to set up another date. I quickly drove to Headquarters and parked. This building happened to be huge. I bristled as I walked toward the entrance. Madison had told me she worked in H&S unit, which was near the front door. As I entered, I saw Madison's unit Logo.

I headed for it and peaked inside. I spotted Madison typing away on the opposite side of the entrance. I stood there until Madison looked up. I motioned for her to come over. As she stood and begin walking over, I noticed that she looked good in her dress uniform. "Hello Everett, what brings you over?"

"I thought I'd come over and get some encouragement from you dear." I softly pinched Madison on the shoulder. "What kind of encouragement Everett?" Madison moved closer. "Hey, you know drill, no kissing in uniform."

"I wasn't going to kiss you silly, I wanted to know what you meant by encouragement." I shuffled my feet a bit before smiling and said, "Look, Madison, I knew what I told you the other night and I've been thinking."

"Yes?"

"Well, I know you're in the dating mode and I wanted to set up another date."

"Sounds good Everett let's try Saturday. You come by the Barracks at 1100 hours, I'll be waiting for you." My spirits picked up and I quickly agreed.

"Well then Madison, I'll see you then."

"Good." Madison motioned for me to leave. I walked away and as I turned around, I saw Madison leaning against the doorpost watching me. For some odd reason I became erect.

When I arrived at the Barracks I noticed the time. It happened to be a little past 1600 hours. I decided to eat chow early and prepare for field day. As I prepared, I begin thinking of Mary. If everything worked out, I knew that I had scheduled to visit Mary and I looked forward to it. All things considered I didn't know how it happened, but I had fallen for Madison. I could feel it in my emotional side. Maybe it was the good sex, whichever the case she was agreeable to my heart. Everyone commenced to field day. It would be some job, cleaning the entire Barracks, but it had become routine now that I had been on the Island several months. My job this evening meant cleaning the head. Several of us had been assigned to this detail. After Corporal Curtis gave us the word we went to work.

As expected, we passed inspection and got Friday off. I had changed into civilian clothing after formation and almost made it to my car before Filson seemingly popped out of nowhere. "What's up player?"

"I'm okay Filson." I didn't want to entertain Filson, not now anyway. I wanted to get to Mary's. Filson egged on the conversation. "Say Walters, you still game?"

"What's the deal Filson you have something for me."

"No, I just wanted you to run an errand for me that's all."

"Where to?"

"Gate Two. It's right near the main street. It's called Lido's. You'll see a sign posted outside the building."

"This better be good Filson!"

"It will be Everett, it will be." I took a rather large packet from Filson and put it in the trunk of my car. I headed for town. I wanted to surprise Mary. She expected me later that evening. I wondered what we'd get into. I drove my car to Gate Two in silence. I wanted to look into the package Filson sent with me, but it had tape wrapped around it and whomever I delivered it too would know it to be tampered with.

I parked in my usual spot away from Gate Two. I took the package and headed for Lido's. When I arrived, I saw a small hole in the wall building with the sign on it. The door was open, so I walked inside. To my surprise, three black men were sitting at a table. One called out,

"You Everett?"

"Yes I am." I said wearily.

"Well, that package you're carrying belongs to me!" He reached out his hand so I gave it to him. I quickly left the joint even before getting a description of the men, but not before the one who spoke thrust a package into my hand. "Damn!" I thought to myself, Filson must have called them before I got here. I begin to wonder what the hell Filson was into. Shaken, I quickly walked back to my car. I wanted to catch Mary at home. It was still early, but you never know what to expect, especially with Mary's hours. I rang the doorbell when I arrived at the home. Yuriko answered. Surprised, I asked if Mary was home. "Yes, one minute please." I stood at the door until Mary came to it. "Walter, you still work at this time, no?"

"I got off early Mary and I thought I'd surprise you." I checked the time; it was not even 0900 hours yet. "This is surprise come in Walter and take off shoes." I took off my sneakers before entering. Mary still had her nightgown on and so did Yuriko, who quickly went into the bedroom. "Well Walter, I was thinking of you coming tonight at Whisper Alley."

"Why what did you have in mind Mary?" The look I gave to Mary said it all.

"Oh, no, not right now Walter, but I want you to do something for me."

"What's that Mary?"

"Go to the Base store and buy some things. I will give you the money." I understood Mary's implications, we had discussed Tuesday, but I didn't think she'd get into it so quickly. "Are you sure you want to start today, Mary?"

"Yes, Walters, now that you come so soon, we can buy and then take them to Whisper Alley tonight."

"I see. And then what?"

"We sell them Walter!" Mary appeared so nonchalant that I almost overlooked what I was doing. The Black Market, from what I had heard was dangerous thing to get into. I wondered how deep did Mary want to take this. Mary left the room in the powder blue see-through gown. I certainly got a full view of everything, but now my mind raced back and forth from Filson and Mary.

For one thing, I hadn't checked the envelope that the black man gave me. I suspected they were military personnel. Those three men at Lido's, if they were indeed military must have been on the Island for some time to be able to hang out at the Club during working hours. Mary came back in the room and handed me a stack of bill. "This is $250 Walter." She then gave me a list. "Buy this and then you bring them back here, okay?"

"No problem, Mary." I said checking the list out. It had a lot of feminine products and meats. I wondered could I pull it off. I said my goodbyes to Mary and then I headed for my car. Once inside, I decided to look in the envelope I received at Lido's. There were ten $20 bills in it. That must have been drugs I reasoned. Filson dealt drugs for someone on the Island. It bugged me because the penalties on the Rock for dealing drugs was harsh and I didn't want to be caught doing so.

I tried to shrug it off as I headed for the commissary on Kadena Air Base. This would be interesting how the cashiers handled my items. When I arrived at the Commissary It wasn't very crowded, so I figured this trip might be a precursor of my next visits. I grabbed a shopping cart and started shopping. The Commissary, huge, had a bit of everything. It took me over an hour, but I had a full shopping cart. When I got to the checkout line, I begin getting a little nervous, but I controlled it very well. The Cashier gave me a funny look, but I understood. The tampons and deodorants and deodorizers, plus all the meat did appear to be out of the ordinary. "Who you shopping for young man?" I had to think of something quick. "My wife and family, we are newlyweds."

"Oh, I see." The Cashier never missed a beat of checking the items. When she finished, she winked at me. I smiled and put everything back in my shopping cart. I had about eight bags of groceries. I packed them into my car and headed out back to Mary's place. I had to admit I had become very nervous, but somehow I held myself in check.

I arrived at Mary's and looked around to see if I was being followed. I was not; I went and knocked on the door, so I could unload the merchandise. Mary opened the door and let me bring in the groceries. "Good, Walters, you buy everything?"

"Yes I did Mary."

"You nervous Walter?"

"Very nervous Mary," but I did it. My poor throat felt like a squad had marched through it. Mary laughed a bit before coming back to the groceries. We got them inside. Mary seemed to see things different now. She appeared to let her guards down, maybe now she felt she could trust me. "Walter, you do me big favor, I want to help you today."

"Okay, Mary, how will you help me?" Mary took me by the hand and led me down the hallway. She took me to a bedroom. As we entered, Yuriko lay there in bed in her bra and panties. Mary let go of my hand

and giggled before saying, "I say you can have anything Walter, and I can tell you like Yuriko." I could feel my blood racing. My penis had filled with blood so quickly I thought it might pop. "Yes Mary I do like her but…" Mary cut me off.

"No, don't say anything Walter, just have a good time." Speechless, I waited for Mary to leave the room. Once she did, Yuriko pulled the covers over her flesh and slid over to give me room to get in the bed. I kept my clothes on as I lay down next to her. We both lay there in silence smiling. I knew this would be something special.

CHAPTER SEVEN
YURIKO

As I lay with Yuriko, I felt a glow that I had never felt before. The young lady was something special. Sure it was ecstatic to be with Madison, very intellectual stimulating, but Yuriko happened to be an exotic woman, something that turned out to be a new experience for me. And I loved it; I caressed her body everywhere. She had such smooth skin and she possessed an ample figure. Her breasts were tout with extremely large nipples. At one point I gently sucked one until it became rock hard. I backed off a bit not wanting to go to fast with Yuriko. I wanted this to last and I didn't want to frighten my turtledove.

While I explored Yuriko's flesh the question kept popping up in my mind. I had to know, "Are you a virgin Yuriko?"

"Yes, I have never slept with a man. I want it to be special Walter." I held Yuriko tightly against me before stating, "I want this to be special too Yuriko." We then gazed into each others' eyes for some time. I gently kissed Yuriko, on the lips at first and then I started probing with my tongue. Yuriko stiffened, but quickly relaxed as the sensations begin to take over her. She giggled and returned the kiss. Not an expert, but it felt good all the same. My poor penis no doubt engorged so with blood couldn't take much more of this. Releasing Yuriko, I suggested we go and talk to Mary. "Okay Walter, I'll do it." I commented to Yuriko on her excellent English. "Thank you Walter, I practice a lot. I want to learn as much English as I can."

"Well, you keep at it, I'm sure you will one day." We both got out of the bed. Yuriko begin pointing at me and giggling. I looked at the direction of her finger. There was a quarter size hole wet spot on my pants. "Oh, it's nothing Yuriko, I like you a lot that's all." Yuriko took my hand and put it between her legs. "Me too Walter." We embraced and kissed again. Yuriko felt good in my arms, I didn't want the moment to stop.

Not very tall, Yuriko probably stood about 5 feet 2 inches tall. Even though I dwarfed her, we still paired rather easily. I liked Yuriko's shape. It resembled the perfect pear. I had to take my mind off of what I wanted to do or I'd end up ripping her clothes off again. Grateful that Yuriko put on her robe, we both went into the main room. Mary had called several people over who were buying the goods Yuriko wanted to go back in the room, but I insisted we stay. Mary noticed us. "Come on Walter and watch me." An older Okinawan gentleman was buying most of the groceries. He appeared to want everything. While he and Mary haggled over the prices, I held Yuriko tight. She seemed to love it; she kept close to me.

After the gentleman left, Mary exclaimed, "I make over $600.00 American Dollars Walter!"

"Whew, that's good Mary, real good." Mary then noticed me holding Yuriko. "You like Yuriko Walter?"

"Yes I do Mary, Yuriko is a very nice girl." Mary nodded at Yuriko before saying, "You two should get married Walter, and you live here." I had to do a double take of what Mary had just said. If I lived here that meant I'd have Yuriko whenever I wanted, but marriage, I was a bit skeptical. I wanted to wait before making such a weighty decision like that. "Listen Mary, I'd love to marry Yuriko and do just that, give me some time okay?"

"You always say, give me some time, but I do, I give you some time to think about it."

"What about you Yuriko?" I said not wanting to leave the precious dove out of it.

"Well I…" Yuriko fell silent and put her arms around my waist. This happened to be a little lady I couldn't refuse. "Yuriko, yes, I'll marry you, but I have to get permission first."

"I understand Walter, but I want to make you feel better."

"You already have Yuriko, by being here." The shy Yuriko buried her face in my chest. Mary appeared to enjoy the scene. "Yes, Walter, anything, remember."

"I remember Mary." I had to admit everything moved so fast now. I had to keep up with things or I'd fall under real quick. I wanted to leave, but Yuriko clung to me without letup. I knew now that she wanted to make love to me, but I wanted to wait just a little bit longer. Let her get real juicy. I had learned a few things over here on the Island about sex and I wanted to begin using them.

I knew that in Nebraska, I happened to be such a moral person and now I acted like a sex fiend. Grandmother warned me of illicit sex and the trap it could become, but I wanted this, it gave me reason to join the Corps. I couldn't stop now. And with this young vixen, ready and willing. At that moment I decided to make love to Yuriko. I took her hand and led her back into the bedroom. First, I quickly undressed; as I took off my briefs, my erection stood tall. Yuriko gasped at my throbbing member. Enjoying every minute of it, I pulled Yuriko's gown off. She stood there waiting for my next move. I uncoupled her bra and removed it. I then slid her panties down to her ankles. Yuriko, smiling and blushing, eagerly stepped out of them. I then gasped at the sight of Yuriko's nakedness. I led her to the bed and guided her to the prone position. This was a special moment for Yuriko, so I wanted to make it count. While Yuriko lay on her back, I began kissing her breasts. I was so horny that I almost couldn't take it, but I wanted it to be just right.

I worked my way down Yuriko's body until I made it to her treasure. Yuriko surprisingly writhed in pleasure. She uttered unintelligible sounds, which clued me that she enjoyed it. I began massaging her clitoris with my tongue very gently so as not to be overwhelming. I worked at it until I could taste Yuriko's bittersweet fluids. She had secreted rather quickly. I then darted my tongue in and out of her love canal. Yuriko couldn't stay still. When I was about to burst, I deftly mounted Yuriko, who quickly parted her legs. I plunged into Yuriko and missed, so Yuriko, anticipating my next moves guided me into her. Surprisingly, I had little trouble thrusting into Yuriko. I systematically began gyrating. The tension built quickly; as I thrust I could feel the climax coming. Despite everything, I started thrusting like a madman. On perhaps the third thrust, I exploded. It felt like a river gushed forth. I shivered as the semen spewed out of me. I clung tightly to Yuriko as I spasmodically jerked. Kissing Yuriko uncontrollably I felt her convulse and then go limp. I lay there on top of her, totally spent. I stayed inside of the glove tight Yuriko. I couldn't keep my hands still. When I finally pulled out, I looked down and sure enough there was blood. Her Hymen had still been intact; I broke her virginity.

Saddened a bit, I realized now that perhaps I was responsible for Yuriko. I didn't quite think sex from Mary would satisfy me right now after making love to Yuriko. Sweating profusely Yuriko spoke. "Walter, we need to take a shower."

"You want to shower together Yuriko?"

"Yes, after our making love I want you to shower with me Walter." I allowed Yuriko to lead me into the restroom. After showering I enjoyed the rest of the afternoon with both Mary and Yuriko. Mary's other daughter arrived from school. I thought that this would be a good time to excuse myself, so I did. "Walter, when you come back?" Mary questioned. "Sunday, Mary," I said. I went and gave Yuriko a great big hug and kissed her before saying goodbye. Such innocence, I couldn't believe they still existed like this. As I left the home, I felt totally rejuvenated. Leaving Mary's now I cold totally concentrate on Filson.

Filson had sort of left me hanging. I had unknowingly delivered drugs for him; at least I wanted to confront him about it. As I drove it seemed like the scales were lifted off my eyes. I noticed passersby's observing me with keen interest. I relished it, especially the young girls. I held my head high basking in the feeling. When I arrived at Base, it was 2300 hours. I knew I couldn't dominate Filson I had to be discrete and take it easy. Don't be alarmed or blow his cover. Even though I didn't understand the whole component of the criminal world, I had a degree of knowledge about things.

The Barracks were empty, no Filson, so I decided to go back downstairs to the snack room and get a snack. When I got down there I had to take a double take. Cameko of all people was here at the Barracks, and to my shock, with Sergeant Larsen. Amazed I played along with Cameko's in acting as though we were strangers. I still nonetheless could feel her eyes burning a hole in me. Out of curiosity I walked up to Larsen. "Hey Sergeant Larsen, what's up?"

"I'm good Walters, what you up too?"

"Not a whole lot why do you ask Sergeant I'm curious."

"Well, this young lady here is looking for you Walters."

"She's not with you Sergeant Larson?"

"No she isn't." I looked at Cameko and instantly felt remorse. "Hi Cameko, how are you?" She didn't answer she only walked outside the Barracks.

"Good luck kid!" Larsen yelled out as I walked out after Cameko. Once outside, I popped the question. "Cameko, what are you doing here?" Cameko looked at me in anger and yelled, "Why you talk to Mary Walter!" Taken aback, I reached in my memory for an answer.

"To be honest Cameko I saw you with another American, so I broke it off."

"You like Mary?"

"Yes I do Cameko, I like her very much." Cameko seemed to calm down a bit before responding, "Yeah, I have new boyfriend, I have many boyfriend, but I thought you different Walter." Cameko appeared to get a little emotional but steadied herself. "Walter, you have car now huh."

"Yes, Cameko I do."

"I need ride back to my place." I started feeling like a taxi and delivery boy at the same time. Plus, I couldn't risk losing Yuriko; I didn't know how she would respond to my seeing Cameko. "Look, Cameko, I can give you a ride, but that's it, no fooling around okay."

"Why, little boy Walter like Mary pussy better than mine!" I didn't answer but I walked toward my car. Cameko followed suit. In the car on the way over to Gate Two, Cameko begin to talk. "Walter, you buy things for Mary?" Trapped, I tried to ignore Cameko. She persisted. Finally I agreed. "Yes, I do Cameko."

"You like Yuriko is that it Walter?" Angered by the inquisitive bitch, but apprehensive about where she got the information, I answered her. "Yes Cameko very much."

"Walter, Okinawan girl different from American girl, you can have all the girls you want she won't be mad."

"But I'm not like that Cameko."

"Oh, you good boy never cheat."

"Well, Cameko, you said it yourself, you have many boyfriends."

"I do, I have to pay rent you know."

"I understand Cameko." She then broke out a small bottle and opened it and quickly drank it. "What's that Cameko?"

"They call it Bron, it will keep you busy."

"Oh really."

"You can buy at Japanese drug store."

"I see. What does it do?"

"Give you energy." As interesting as that sounded, I planned to ignore it, but you never know.

"Walter, I used to work at Whisper Alley." Not surprised, still I let the comment soak in. I thought Cameko to be a hustler, but not, Whisper Alley, she didn't seem tough enough. "Oh really?"

"Yes, for six months. Then I stop. Too much Fucke, fucke." I laughed at Cameko's way of saying it.

"What's so funny Walter?"

"Your speech about sex."

"Well I have to work Whisper Alley."

"Why Cameko?"

"Yakuza." That name began popping up again. I heard Tucker telling me never to mention it, but now Cameko said it. "Are you afraid of Yakuza Cameko?"

"You should be too Walter, they are dangerous people. They control Gate Two and Whisper Alley."

"Is that so?"

"Yes, and don't tell anyone but they watch you Walter because you move from girl to girl quickly."

"And?"

"Well now that you and Mary are Black Market, you okay they like that." So here I was waist deep in illegal activities and now Cameko tells me I'm being watched. I wondered about Filson and that package he had me deliver. Did he have ties to this Yakuza? I shuddered at the thought. Damn, Filson may have been in way over his head. And what was he doing with the money he earned. I heard stories of how Naval Investigation kept close tabs on lawbreakers. Okinawa, only so big being that it's an Island, it would be easy to keep tabs on one Marine that is unless Filson turned out to be more calculated than I gave him credit for being. Cameko did most of the talking on the way over. Deep in thought, I mechanically drove toward Gate Two Street, all the while observing Cameko. She became fidgety as ever scratching and rubbing herself. Finally I got her to her apartment. "Want to come inside Walter?"

"Yes, Cameko we need to talk."

"Okay, you come inside we talk." I parked my car and followed Cameko to the apartment. I watched her unlock the door and open it. She motioned for me to come in, so I followed her into the darkened home. When Cameko turned on the dim lights, four black men sat in her living room and to my surprise there was Filson, who spoke first. "My man Walters, come and sit down have a seat." Nervous, but confident, I walked into the small sparsely furnished room and had a seat on a small stool. Filson seemed relaxed, that's when I noticed the marijuana cigarette in his hand. Yep, it was the unmistakable aroma of weed. "Take a hit Marine!"

"No thanks Filson."

"Take a hit!" Not knowing what else to do I took the cigarette and inhaled. Not a smoker of course I coughed the smoke right back out. "Hit it again!" Which I did; Filson laughed as he took the joint from me. "I see you've met my bitch Cameko, huh, Walters."

"Some time ago Filson, now what's this all about?"

"What's this all about! Why I'm surprised at you Walters, don't you know?"

"No I don't Filson."

"Well let me tell you. You've just been chosen as my runner. I need something transported you deliver that clear!" It was a statement not a question, so I didn't answer. "You see Walters, those three big mean niggers here. They work for me, you do what you're told and we'll be fine, if not, well we can easily find you Walters. One of us will find you." Filson then tried to reassure me. "And besides Walters there's money in it for everyone." As he said that one man stood. A massive individual, black skinned with a baldhead, walked up to me and smiled and without warning he gut punched me in the stomach. With no air in my lungs, I crumbled to the floor. I must have passed out because when I awakened they were gone. Cameko stood over me as I caught my breath. "You okay Walter?"

"No, but I'll manage." Cameko let me get up by myself. When I looked in her eyes I could sense the smirk. Cameko had set me up. Filson had me right where he wanted me. Going to the authorities might be dangerous, so I quickly dismissed the thought. As I thought the worst was over, two Okinawan men came into the room. Dizzy from the cannabis, I stayed on the floor. The men smiled and handed me a picture of Yuriko. Afterwards they quickly left.

Cameko laughed, smiled and said, "you see Walter, now you tell, they hurt Yuriko." Hurt and heartbroken, I knew I would have to do what is that Filson wanted. I had heard of premonitions, but this was too much. Cameko handed me a bottle of Bron. Without hesitating I grabbed it and drank it. I didn't care at this point. I felt like a trapped animal with nowhere to turn. How did I get into this nightmare? The car! I realized a car that nice could only spell trouble. And with the Marine Corps knowing my dad as an Army Officer, I played right in his hands.

He knew I had the golden boy image. Well, the way I felt about Yuriko I'd do anything now. The Bron brought me back to life. The pain had left my stomach. Cameko had stripped to her panties and now lay on the couch. My world as I knew it had changed.

As I steadied myself, Filson entered the room. "Let's go Walters, let's get back to Base." Filson thought about it before adding, "wait here Walters. I have some unfinished business to take care of. He walked toward Cameko and then ripped off her panties. Filson quickly dropped his pants and begin screwing the all too willing whore who begged for more. Strangely enough I became erect at the spectacle. As I watched Filson screw Cameko, I understood a bit about the warnings I received about Whisper Alley. It was more than sex it was a culture. The thing that could befall a man, especially a naïve one such as myself could be ruinous. Perhaps twenty minutes later after much yelling pumping and screaming, Filson got up and wiped himself with Cameko's panties. She lay there breathing hard, but she appeared content. Filson took out some bills and laid them on the couch. "Let's roll Walters!" I walked out of the small place ahead of Filson not bothering to look toward the diabolical Cameko.

Once we were inside my car, Filson began explaining his stand on the matter. "Look, Walters, you are the talk of Camp Kinser. With this shiny new ride and all you are known by almost everyone. Now we all know about your daddy and his pull. And to be honest Walters, you are a valuable man to have." I drove, but I remained silent; Filson went on, "Oh, you can snitch if you want, but knowing you, I don't think that's an issue. Besides that pretty little Okinawan and W.M. have you right where I want you." Filson laughed, a hard demonic laugh. I cringed at the thought. I had unknowingly become a criminal. Still, I had my integrity. When we arrived on Camp Kinser, I calmly got out of the car, waited for Filson to get out and as I waited for him to come to my side, I punched him in the stomach. Filson tried to inhale and went on one knee. "We're even Filson!" I said as I headed into the Barracks, not bothering to look back.

CHAPTER EIGHT
SATURDAY

I met Madison as planned. We both ate breakfast on Base before meeting at the W. M. Barracks. Madison looked cute today. She wore a nice light yellow knee length dress with a halter-top. Okinawa, a place that got cold but not freezing, which evidently Madison understood. "Hey Mr. Walters how are you?"

"I'm fine Madison, nice day isn't it, yes, nice day for a stroll through the city."

"I think so sir." The December breeze reminded me that I should have a jacket, but watching Madison I decided to brave the storm. "Hey Madison, let's get in the car okay?"

"Wait, I have to get something from the Barracks, I'll be right back."

"I'll be in the car." Madison exited and quickly went into the Barracks. A little chilly I went and sat in the car. I tried to piece together what had taken place last night. It almost felt like a dream, yet the horror of what had happened gripped me like steel vice. I knew that I wanted Yuriko very badly even though Love may not have been the right word, attachment probably fit better. I remembered Cameko's words: "Okinawan women let their men fool around." Now while I disliked what Cameko did, I had become violently inflamed watching her and Filson screw. The way Cameko responded to the animal sex enthralled me, I actually wanted her, but I knew that Mary would find out.

Filson was in something very deep, I could tell. He never said anything else to me even after the punch I planted on him. I saw him at chow and he even winked at me, strange indeed. Right now I'd deal with it. I had 8 months left on the Rock, and then I'd see what transpired. I waited for what seemed like hours and Madison finally came out.

"Sorry for taking so long Everett, but I had business to take care of." Madison jumped in the car. "Where to Madison?"

"Oh, I thought we'd go for a cruise, I'd love to see a little bit of Okinawa."

"I have a better idea, why don't we visit a friend of mine, Jonah Crockett, I have to call him first though." Hesitant at first, but Madison finally agreed.

"Okay, but we can't over stay our welcome can we?"

"We'll be fine Madison, I promise." I got out of the car and went to the phone booth outside of the W. M. Barracks. I reached into my wallet to pull out Jonah's number. When I called Monique answered the phone. "Hello,"

"Hello, this is Everett Walters, I'm a friend of Jonah's, is he there?"

"Yes, one moment, I'll get him for you." Moments later Jonah answered the phone. "Hey Walters what's shaking."

"I'm fine Jonah, hey listen, I'd like to come to your home, but I need the address."

"Where are you now Walters?"

"I'm at Camp Kinser."

"Well we're down the Street at the Base Housing Complex. I tell you what, I'll be at the gate waiting for you is that alight?"

"Sure, that will be fine Jonah."

"Alright see you then." I went back to the car and got in. We took off for Jonah's. Madison had something to get off her chest. "Listen, Everett, I have something I want to say."

"Yes Madison?"

"You know the thing I told you the other night?"

"I remember Madison."

"Well, I'm trying to start a group here in Okinawa, you interested?"

"First of all, what's involved Madison I have to know."

"I know you think it's a cult, but actually it's a way of worshipping."

"Oh, really; worshipping what?"

"You see, Everett, we believe in the right to worship science. There is no Creator Everett!"

"Do your parents know about your beliefs Madison?" Madison giggled and put her head down; she looked away from me before answering: "no they don't, why do you ask anyway."

"Well Madison, I thought that would be your major concern, what your parents felt about such a thing."

"Screw what my parents think Everett, they're old and out of touch with reality!" I sensed Madison getting upset, so I tried to change the subject. "Hey there's the Base Housing Complex, why don't we try and find Jonah." Still in a huff Madison wasn't through. "Look, Everett, I thought you and I could have a relationship while we did our tour over here on Okinawa, why are you making things so difficult!"

"Madison, I'm only trying to understand. I believe in God okay, I'm having a little bit of trouble understanding you right now." I wheeled the car into the Complex. I spotted Jonah right away. He quickly went to his car, so I followed him.

We went through the rather large complex unimpeded. We quickly got to the non-rate section. The units looked pretty nice from my vantage point, not bad. Madison also appeared impressed. "Hey, Everett, you want to get married?"

"Sure, when you start believing in God!"

"That's not fair Everett, it's a free Country you know and I am American."

"I'm only kidding Madison, besides, you're not serious either." Jonah pulled up to a unit and got out of his car. He motioned for me to park on the street near his unit. Both Madison and I got out of my car and approached Jonah. "Nice wheels Walters, how long have you had it?"

"About 5 months Jonah, you know I kind of like that old Chevy you're driving too."

"Well I bought it from an Air Force Sergeant, got it kind of cheap."

"I see,"

"Hey, why don't you two come inside."

"By the way Jonah, this is my friend Madison."

"Hello Madison, I'm Jonah." Jonah took Madison's hand. "Nice to meet you, Jonah." We then all went inside, Monique was there waiting to greet us. "So you're the famous Everett Walters."

"At your service Mam."

"Come here you." I went to Monique and she gave me a big hug. "Jonah has told me so much about you, I don't know where to start."

"Don't I kind of like it that way." Monique let go of my hand.

"Who's your friend?"

"Monique, this is Madison Bilkens."

"Hello Madison, how are you?"

"I'm just fine," Madison said. She coolly reached out her hand to Monique, who vigorously shook Madison's hand. "Look, everyone, I hate to leave, but I have to get to work." Jonah encouraged us to have a seat. "You two make yourselves comfortable right here on the couch. I led Madison to the couch and we sat sown. "Before I go can I get you two anything to drink?"

"We're fine, thanks Monique."

"Well, it's nice meeting the both of you, especially you Mr. Walters, now I can tell all of my friends how handsome Jonah's friend is."

"Oh, I bet you say that to all the guys."

"Only when it's true." Monique excused herself and Jonah followed close behind. I made a mental picture of Monique, she happened to be a stunningly beautiful woman, no wonder Jonah put up such a fuss.

She happened to be halfway through her pregnancy. When we were alone, I looked around the home. Very well organized. Jonah had taste I could see that. They even had a large screen television. Madison seemed to like what she saw as well. "You could really get comfortable here Everett, very comfortable." Madison looked over at me and winked. I didn't want to lead her on, but still I toyed with the idea of a relationship with her. Jonah quickly came back into the apartment. "You know Everett, Monique and I have things to take care of, she has to work and I need to go to Base up in Hansen, but you know Walters, we have an extra bed, we're waiting on the baby." Jonah winked at me and said, "you are welcome to use it until we get back." Madison said nothing; she pretended not to hear Jonah. "Look, Jonah," I said, "maybe now is not a good time."

"Don't be silly Walters, now is as good a time as any. The room is down the hall to the right. Hey we better got moving. See you in a couple of hours." Jonah departed leaving us alone. "Well what do you think Madison?"

"It's fine Everett, I'd like to lie down for a while and unwind. I wish we had something to drink; I'm dying to relax a little. I was up all night studying about evolution."

"Well let me see if Jonah has beer in the Fridge."

I got up and went to the Fridge and checked inside. There was no beer, but there were two bottles of wine unopened; I took one and then I looked for and found two cups. I went back into the guest room with Madison, "Ahh, alas my dove, I found a cure for ailment."

"Oh, Everett, you're so romantic, let's go into the bedroom and drink okay?"

"Sure, Madison, why not." We went into the bedroom and looked inside. There was hardly room for the bed and not much else. I noticed the unit was a nice off blue shade of paint. "Boy, the rooms are sure small." Madison whispered.

"I know Madison, but it's the thought that counts remember."

"You're right Everett why should I complain. Anyway, I do need to relax." I handed Madison a cup and poured a half glass of wine. "You sure opened that fast Everett, I didn't notice you open it."

"Well, I tried to hide it from you." Madison shrugged her shoulders and begin drinking the wine. I decided I didn't want to have a drink, so I sat my cup down on the small black dresser. "Aren't you going to have a drink Everett?"

"No I better not Madison, I need to stay focused, you go ahead and enjoy yourself." Actually I knew how easy alcoholism was and I didn't dare risk becoming dependent on the sauce. Madison held out her glass for more. Silently I poured her another glass. She also drank in silence. Moments later after draining the juice, Madison stripped down to her bra and panties. "Everett, I need to take a nap. I'm very relaxed now."

"So are you saying you want to be alone?"

"Well, you can lie down with me, but I don't want sex okay Everett, I'm serious."

"Sure Madison anything you say angel." To be honest, I was relieved; Yuriko had pushed my button last night. I unloaded the load of the century. I might get erect, but I was totally satisfied.

I stripped to my skivvies and jumped in bed with Madison. She was soft to the touch; it felt good holding her in my hands and being so close together. Madison seemed to be dozing off. "You know Everett?"

"Yes Madison!"

"Remember you told me to wait for you?"

"I remember saying that, Madison."

"Well, I met this guy the night after Tuesday and I had sex with him." Surprised, I tried to stay calm: "Really Madison?"

"Yes, and now I'm a bit sore, he was very aggressive and I wasn't ready for him. He had a huge member, wide and long."

"Who was it, Madison?"

"I met him at the E-Club, his last name is Thorn." I didn't get angry, but I patted Madison on her pillow soft rear end." "So you're saying you like messing around?" Madison turned around in the bed and faced me: "Yes, Everett, I like fooling around, I want to explore my body and Thorn was there when you weren't, I'm sorry Everett!"

"That's okay Madison, no strings attached remember?"

"Yes," Then almost instantly Madison dozed off. I guess the liquor was the truth serum. I let her sleep as I caressed her. Erect as ever I couldn't help myself; I decided to try and sleep a bit myself.

Several hours later, I woke up to Madison playing violently with my tool. I awakened just as she brought me to climax. Madison jumped as the liquid gushed forth. "Goodness Everett, you really had a load." Madison got up and left the room. Seconds later, she came back with some toilet tissue and tried to clean the mess up. "Everett, I may have become pregnant with that much semen."

"Well, Madison, you know how to bring it out."

"That I do, Everett, that I do!"

"Hey, let's get dressed and go to the guest room, how about it."

"Okay." I wasn't in the mood for love not right now anyway. Madison, as honest as she had been, didn't hurt my feelings, but I had started to lose desire for her.

Thorn was low class to say the least and him of all people. I didn't want to confront Madison about it, let it go, I'd tell her later that maybe we should stop seeing each other; maybe it was all a mistake. But, on second thought, I still could have her has a steady, especially considering what Cameko said about fidelity. If that were true, Yuriko would not question my moves. Actually, Yuriko would do just fine as far as a lover, but Madison intrigued me. Right then and there I decided to share her with whomever she wanted to screw.

We went back into the living room after Madison folded the sheets that I soiled. We tried watching the Far East Network television that was available to Military personnel, but it wasn't that interesting. Madison looked me over then questioned me: "Do you miss Nebraska much Everett?"

"Sure, don't you Madison? I mean I realize that it's not Chicago, or New York, but it's home."

"What do you like most about Lincoln Everett?" I carefully chose my words. "Madison, I like the history of Nebraska as well, it's very colorful you know. Where should I begin? Madison did you know that in the 1500's, the Pawnee Indians first lived in the land before it being called Nebraska?"

"No, I didn't know that Everett, but I do know that Nebraska has very unusual animals."

"I'll say, Madison, what about the chickadee, you ever heard of it!"

"Somewhat, but not a whole lot." Madison seemed to be churning her thoughts reaching for knowledge. "Everett, Nebraska, does have a rich history, ever since it was repurchased in 1803 with the Louisiana Purchase."

"You're right Madison, but did you know a Mammoth discovered near Lincoln caused Nebraska to be the first State to choose an official fossil?"

"You know Everett, a lot of people put Nebraska down, but with our agricultural strength, American wouldn't be the same without us!"

"You're absolutely right Madison, but you know, even though I didn't necessarily like him, Malcolm Little, is from Omaha Nebraska."

"Yes, Everett, I really admired him for trying to help displaced blacks find themselves in life, Lord knows someone had to do it." I nodded my head at the grim reality, although thinking of Filson gave me the impression that blacks knew more than they let on. "What's your favorite food in Lincoln Madison?"

"I liked Valentino's Pizza and Poppycock popcorn, not to mention Grandpa Jack's Hot Sauce."

"Yeah, that brings back memories. Well Madison, our pioneer way of life proves one thing!"

"What's that Everett?"

"That we're not living up to our reputation of having strong morals."

"Well, I'll do better when I get home. By the way where did you live in Lincoln Everett?"

"I lived at 2317 Garland Street, near Leighton Ave, with my grandmother, Margaret Walters. I didn't want to travel with my father who is an Army Colonel I wanted stability. My grandmother promised me her home, but I hope she lives a long time, so I can visit with her."

"I see; you never told me your dad is a Colonel!"

"Oh, yes, that's part of the reason I joined the Military, dad introduced me to it and I liked the camaraderie and travel."

"But I thought you said you didn't want to travel with your dad?"

"Not as a kid, but as an adult, it's a different story."

"Well, Everett, I used to live on the other side of town on Freemont Street."

"You know Madison, do you plan on going to school once you're discharged?"

"Maybe, I'm not sure." Madison looked over at me, smiled and patted me on the thigh.

Jonah then walked into the home. He seemed surprised to see us in a vertical position, but said nothing about it. "Hello you two, sorry I took so long, but I'm going to the rifle range next month, so I had to make preparations for it."

"I understand Jonah, hey listen, Madison and I want to travel a bit on the Island, so if you'll excuse us." Madison and I stood up and prepared to leave; Jonah interrupted us:

"You don't want to stay for dinner?"

"Well, Jonah, we really want to see the Island before the day is over."

"Sure, my friend anytime."

"By the way Jonah, we used some of your wine and left the bottle in the bedroom, is that alright?"

"You owe me Walters, now I'm definitely looking toward your rain check." I shook Jonah's hand and then led Madison out of the unit. I felt relaxed despite myself. Madison really relieved the tension. We jumped into the car. "Where to young lady?"

"Actually, I just wanted to go for a ride Everett!"

"I tell you what Madison, let's go to Naha and watch a movie."

"Deal Everett, I'd like that." I thought of the Ryukyu Islands and its history. At the moment I wasn't up for touring today facing angry Okinawan people who resented our presence on the Island. America had totally dominated the natives, however, I was amazed at how well the Okinawans recovered after the major wars and American returning the control of the Islands back to Japan. Naha looked like any other bustling city.

I drove down the main Street in Naha and turned on a side Road going into the shopping mall. It was busy but I found a parking spot; Madison and I would take a stroll and sights see a minute and then check out a Movie. It seemed like the natural thing to do today. As we strolled together, I couldn't help but be impressed by Jonah. The man certainly had a plan, and Monique turned out to be a goddess. I didn't know Jonah had it in him.

Visiting the unit gave me an idea about marriage. I wanted Yuriko, she had my number, but Madison was turning out to be a real sweetheart despite herself. As we ducked into the mall with the theater, I could not enjoy myself thinking of Filson. He really ruined my plans that I had made for myself. Now I was a lawbreaker in the making. I wanted to keep it as low profile as possible. After about 15 minutes of walking, we spotted the movie hall. "Come on Madison, let's see what's playing!"

"I hope they have something in English Everett, it's not much fun watching a foreign film if you know what I mean."

"Who's coming for the movie Madison." I jokingly patted on the rear. As I looked around several Okinawan men were soaking up Madison's long thick legs. I chuckled as we ducked into the theater.

CHAPTER NINE
HARD CORE

That Monday morning after chow, I decided to go to Lieutenant Wikenberg, and man-to-man tell him about the possibility marriage between Yuriko and I. I knew the Lieutenant liked me not only because of my father, but my work ethic while stationed here on the Island happened to be tremendous. I did everything that they asked of me and then some. My promotion to corporal was due next week. I knew being promoted to Corporal meritorious would be a possibility.

After formation I requested to speak to the Lieutenant. Sergeant Larsen granted it and I sat facing the C.O. "What's on your mind son?"

"Sir, to be perfectly honest I want to get some information about the possibility of marriage!"

"Is that so lance corporal?"

"Yes, sir!"

"Son let me tell you a little about Okinawan women. First of all, does she work in a Bar?"

"No sir, she never has. She's seventeen sir."

"Hmmm, so you lucked out and found a proper girl, huh Walters?"

"With all due respect sir, I have."

"Well, I'll tell you what you need to know son. This isn't United States by any stretch of the imagination and these women, although not as bad as other places, want to put their hooks in a serviceman and get to good ole U.S. of A. and son, once you're married you have to realize that not everyone will approve of you with an Okinawan." I tried to keep my composure. The Lieutenant had some valid points, but he didn't know the whole story and Lord knows I couldn't explain things the way they actually were. So I bid for time. "Sir, I really like Yuriko, she's a very well mannered and nice girl. I don't foresee any trouble." Wikenburg leaned back in his chair and laughed. "They never are trouble until you meet the family!"

"Sir, how do you know so much about marriage to Okinawans?"

"Well son, I married one six months ago!" Stunned, I remained silent. The Lieutenant may know people in my circle and if so, I was in deep water. The Lieutenant and I exchanged glances for several moments before he said: "Look Walters, if you are determined to marry this individual named Yuriko be my guest. Although you need to talk to the Company C.O. and then the Chaplin."

"Yes sir!"

"Dismissed lance corporal; and oh, by the way, get ready for your promotion next week."

"Yes sir! Sir Lance Corporal Walters request permission to speak with company C.O.?"

"Permission granted, be back here at 1300 hours Marine!"

"Yes sir!" I quickly stood and did an about face. Then I headed toward the company.

At 1200 hours I had the C.O.'s blessing. The Chaplin wanted to know a date so I told him in two weeks. He set up an appointment for that Saturday. After eating chow, I headed back to the Motor Pool.

I got there a bit early, so I sat under the front of the shop under the tin roof. To my surprise Filson came over. "Hey Walters, what's shaking baby?"

"I'm good Filson, you?"

"Cool man, I'm cool. Hey look Marine I need you to run a package for me tonight."

"Where to Filson?"

"To Cameko's house, she knows and she'll let you in."

"How long have you known Cameko Filson?"

"Oh, about a year, we're off and on you know what I mean, she just a side kick Walters."

"I see, so you're not in love I take it."

"With her, hell no, she's a sex freak; she'll do it anytime anyplace."

"Well, I was just checking." Filson looked around before saying: "look deliver this package and there's a grand in it for you." I remained silent but nodded my head. I realized that my agreeing with Filson spelled safety for me. "You'll be alright Walters just follow what I tell you to do." Filson walked away in his usual manner. No one really questioned or jerked around with Filson. I was curious and I'd ask Corporal Curtis when I got the chance. I went and reported to Sergeant Larsen, who gave me a trip ticket. I had a run over to Supply to take supplies to Hansen again. This time I'd ride solo.

I got back to Base around 1730 hours. I secured the vehicle, turned in my trip ticket and headed for the Barracks. I showered and dressed then I headed for the door. Filson sat waiting for me by my car. "I thought you'd never get here Walters." Filson waited for me to get in the car and went under his shirt and pulled out a medium sized packet. "Like I said earlier today Walters, take this to Cameko and pick up your money from her." Filson dropped the packet in my lap and walked away.

A little perturbed, but nonetheless I put the packet under my seat. As I headed out, I knew that if I were caught I'd take the fall, Filson had set it up that way. Whoever they worked for must have really thought things through. When I was waved through the gate by the Military Police, I was slightly shaking. Relieved that they passed me through I concentrated on Yuriko. I would tell her I planned to marry her in two weeks, so she'd better be ready. I wanted to stay with Yuriko for less than an hour and I wanted to get rid of the package as soon as possible. The night air was a welcome relief to the nauseated feeling I had. I dare not look in the package it would not set well with the person receiving it. No, I'd leave it alone.

As I drove up to Mary's home, she opened the front door and came outside to greet me. "Walter, why you come so late I have been waiting for you!"

"Sorry Mary, but I had to work."

"I go to Whisper Alley now you stay and talk with Yuriko."

"Look Mary there's something I need to tell you."

"Yes Walter?"

"I have permission to Marry Yuriko and we're scheduled in two weeks." Mary ran to me and hugged me. "This is good Walter, I'm happy now. You go inside to tell Yuriko, okay?"

"Yes, Mary, I'll do that." As Mary walked away, I walked into the home. Yuriko met me and walked into my arms. A quiet girl, yet Yuriko exploded with emotions. "Hello Yuriko."

"Hi Walter." We lightly kissed then I looked Yuriko in the eyes. "Listen Yuriko, I want to marry you, do you want to get married?"

"Yes, Walter, I do."

"Great!" I yelled, my spirits had picked up like a stiff breeze blowing a feather. "Yes, Yuriko this is great we will be happy together."

"I know Walter, I'm happy now."

"Me too, Yuriko; hey listen I'll let you know when so I can come and get you alright."

"When are we getting married Walter?"

"In two weeks, Yuriko aboard Camp Kinser."

"Aboard?"

"That means we will be on the Base Yuriko."

"Oh, Yuriko smiled knowing she had learned a new word. I hugged her tight before leaving. "I need to run an errand Yuriko and I'll see you tomorrow."

"Where are you going Walter?"

"I need to deliver something very important, do you want me to come back?"

"I'll go with you." That did it; Yuriko was putting her hooks in me already. I gave in not wanting to upset her. "What about your little sister?"

"She's okay. She's asleep, I won't stay long will I Walter."

"No you won't Yuriko." We went and got into my car. Cameko's home was right around the corner. As we parked Yuriko looked around quite vigorously. "Who do you know here Walter?"

"I'm supposed to deliver a packet to Cameko." Yuriko didn't question me any further she remained silent. "Will you please sit in the car until I get back Yuriko?"

"Yes, Walter, I will." I deftly took the packet and without shielding it I took it out of the car. I walked to Cameko's door and knocked on it. Cameko answered the door and ushered me in. "Hi Walter, I supposed to get something from you!" I handed her the packet. "You want to stay Walter?"

"Not tonight Cameko, maybe next time." Cameko smiled and went into a room. Seconds later she came back with an envelope. "This is for you Walter." I took the envelope and looked into it. Money; I took out some of it and handed it to Cameko. "For next time okay Cameko?"

"Okay." I caressed her body before I left the apartment. For some reason I was wildly excited by the scene of Cameko and Filson the other night, I knew I'd be back.

I made it back to Yuriko: "So where do you want to go Yuriko?"

"I'd like to go to your Base."

"I'll take you there someday soon, but not tonight, Yuriko." Yuriko appeared not to get upset, but she didn't say anything. "I tell you what Yuriko, I'll visit with you tonight okay?" Yuriko smiled and nodded her head. I then took notice of her. She was wearing a short blue dress and white loose-fitting top. With Filson's packet on my mind my arousal was affected, but after looking at Yuriko the desire flashed forth again.

We went to Mary's house and went inside. Yuriko led me to her room and we both sat down on the bed. "You like to make love Walter?"

"Yes, Yuriko I do!" Yuriko put her hand on my knee and started: "Me too Walter, but I'm still sore from last time we had sex."

"I'm sorry Yuriko, I never figured I'd be so rough."

"Let's just hold each other okay Walter?"

"That sounds great Yuriko I don't mind holding you tonight." We lay down on the bed embracing each other. I must have been tired because no sooner had I stretched out I dozed off.

Shaken awake by Yuriko, I looked at my watch, 0200 hours. I quickly sat up in bed, "Walter, you go to Base now okay, it's late!"

"Yes Yuriko I will." I awkwardly got out of bed and stood up. I remembered the rumor that Orientals slept on the floor. I dismissed the thought, kissed Yuriko and methodically left the house. I had become violently inflamed while embracing the silky Yuriko. I decided to visit Mary at Whisper Alley. I wanted to test Mary and see if she meant what she said about "anything." I drove my car right up to the Air Force base and parked it. Because of the time, I wanted to be quick about things. I made it to Whisper Alley in a few minutes; it was very deserted when I arrived. I went to Mary's door and there was Mary waiting. "Hey, Mary!"

"Hi Walter, what are you doing here?"

"I came to see you again just like old times."

"You want short time?" I hesitated a bit before adding:

"Yes I do." Mary mischievously smiled and invited me in. "I don't have much time, Mary."

"Okay, we do short time Walter." Mary led me into the room. I handed her a twenty. She quickly got out of her clothes and I did the same. "Hi." Mary exclaimed, "You very horny Walter!"

"Yes!" I whispered as I jerked at Mary's fondling my ever-stiffening erection. Mary, with my penis in hand led me to the bed. I mounted her and she guided me in to her vagina. I had so much tension that I didn't thrust very long before I exploded. I tried to penetrate as deep as possible, but my discharge wouldn't let me. Mary giggled as she received my fluids. When I tried to get up, Mary held me: "No, not yet you not finished!" I lay on top of Mary getting everything out of my climax. "Walter, you no make love to Yuriko?"

"She didn't feel good Mary and I do remember you saying, 'anything' so I came here."

"You have good memory Walter." Mary finally released me and I stood. She carefully wiped my still erect but sensitive organ. "You sleep good tonight, Walter, you very horny tonight."

"This is true Mary and thanks."

"That's okay Walter, you come to my house soon okay?"

"Yes I will Mary very soon, I'll bring you some liquor next time."

"Okay I wait." Mary kissed me on the cheek and then said: "I won't tell Yuriko, Walter."

"I appreciate that Mary, thanks again." I dressed all the while trying to keep Mary's hands off me. Finally I dressed and departed the Alley from a giggling Mary. I made it to the Barracks at around 0230 hours. I thanked God that I didn't drink regularly.

The next day at work I finally got Corporal Curtis alone. We had taken an m880 to refuel on Base. "Listen Corporal Curtis, what's the deal with Filson?"

"He's a shit bird Walters, and I do mean shit bird. But at the same time, he does his work and he stays on line. One thing is he being from the streets, you never know what he's thinking."

"Does he have connections with anyone?" Curtis looked at me: "why do you want to know Walters?"

"Well I just thought he presented himself more than meets the eye that's all."

"Walters, you have a car and you probably have women, why are you concerned with a Marine like Filson anyway?"

"I'm not, I'm curious that's all."

"I wouldn't recommend that you try asking him that I hear he's good with his fist." I thought of the lanky well-built Filson. He probably could have passed for a middle weight boxer. "Believe me Corporal, I won't."

"Good, now what's this about you getting married?"

"Oh, I'm getting hitched in two weeks, to a fine girl. Her name is Yuriko." Curtis nodded and continued to drive the pickup. I wasn't satisfied with the information he gave me, but I had to accept it right now not having anything else to rely on.

That evening after work I hooked up with Dunbar and we worked out together. Afterwards we decided to go to the E-Club. Dunbar, at this time was deeply involved with Natalie Hunter, a decent Woman Marine, but a bit immature, although she genuinely liked the diminutive Dunbar: "Hey Dunbar, you still having trouble with Thorn?"

"No, but I hear he's porking some woman named Madison." Struck by the comment yet I continued. "Yeah, that's what I hear too!" Dunbar looked at me incredulously:

"She's your girl Walters, aren't you going to dismember the Bastard!"

"No Dunbar, and she's not my girl, we're good friends that's all."

"That's not what I hear. Word is that you're in love and she leading you on." Dunbar chuckled at the insult. "Where the hell did you hear that from Dunbar!" I couldn't believe the shit that circulated around the Base. "Walters, Natalie told me and she heard it right from Madison." Madison must have felt that way because of my good-natured personality that I had fell for her. "What else did you hear Dunbar?"

"Oh, that she didn't like Thorn, but she only wanted to see where your head was in the relationship."

"I see, now does she expect me to try begging for her?"

"You'd have to ask her that Walters." I took the advice bitterly, but remained silent. We entered the Club. It was very crowded tonight; it appeared to be a Western night again. "Damn, Dunbar, it looks like we're in right on time!"

"Yes, as a matter of fact, look!" Dunbar pointed over to Madison and Thorn all hugged up in a corner. To be truthful I didn't give a damn, but I said: "I'll be darn Dunbar, you're right, she likes Mr. Thorn."

"I wouldn't lie to you friend." Dunbar then excused himself and went to his girl. I stood there staring at Madison hoping she'd look my way, but she didn't. I decided to have a drink. I walked up to the Bar, which was very crowded and took my place in line. Moments later Madison walked by me. She didn't speak, but her eyes contact let me know that she was still busy with Thorn. I realized she desperately wanted to avoid violence between Thorn and I. I took the hint and remained silent. After ten minutes of waiting, I finally got to the counter: "Two Budweiser's please."

"Coming right up." The Barmaid quickly handed me two ice cold Bud's; I paid for them and went and stood against the wall with dozens of other leathernecks. I drank in silence, downing the beers in minutes. I couldn't take much of this, so I went to order some food at the snack bar in the rear of the Club. A line there too!" I patiently waited before I ordered. With my food I headed out of the Club and back to the Barracks. Not wanting to drive on Base at the time, I walked the 5-minute or so walk.

I ate my food in silence and prepared for sleep. No sooner had I got undressed and hit the rack, I had a visitor, it was Filson. Everyone else in the quarters was gone, so Filson walked right in. "Hey Walters, I hear you did a good job delivering my package. Good because I have another one coming up and I want you to be ready."

"Good night, Filson!"

"Good night, Walters." Filson quietly left the quarters; he knew he had my number so raising hell at this point wouldn't make sense. After brainstorming a bit, I checked the time. 2140 hours. I figured what the hell, I'd try and catch Cameko at home and then I'd see what course of action to take. Throwing my clothes back on, I quickly went to my car and jumped in it. Yeah, Cameko had been on my mind for a while. After witnessing she and Filson thrashing around on the couch, I wanted some of Cameko.

I quickly drove to Gate Two Street. I parked out of sight as usual near Cameko's place. I got out of the car and went to her door. I knocked and to my surprise Cameko answered. "Walter, I knew you come back, I waited here for you."

"Hello Cameko." I said and waited for Cameko to invite me in, which she did. She had a see-through pink nightgown on. You could see that she wasn't wearing any panties. I could smell her musky scent. I instantly became erect. "Cameko I just wanted to apologize for not continuing to see you."

"It's okay Walter, you think I'm bad girl now?"

"Well, yes, but I like you that way." Cameko smiled before adding: "You not angry for me coming to your Base and bringing you here for bad men?"

"Yes Cameko, I'm angry, but I wanted to take it out on you in bed." Cameko smiled a bit and unexpectantly pulled her nightgown over her head exposing her nakedness. "Come and get it Walter!" And then she ran for the bedroom. I caught up with her and wrapped my arms around her. It was against all ethical purposes, but I started kissing Cameko. At first on the lips and then I began sticking my tongue down her throat. She responded by giving me hers. Cameko quickly helped me to undress. Seconds later, we both were naked and embracing. Throbbing, I huskily asked, "lay down Cameko!" she responded by going to the bed and pulling the covers back and lying down with her legs spread apart. I lie on top of her and let her guide me in. Remembering Filson I started thrusting violently. Cameko began moaning and trying to return the hip movement. We both began panting and exclaiming while we reached our pinnacles. I came first, then Cameko yelled and then went limp. I continued lightly thrusting while I tried to regain myself. Afterwards I got up and wiped myself with Cameko's gown. She cautiously observed me, but said nothing. I took out $100 and threw it on the bed. I began dressing with Cameko's scent on me. I headed for the door: "Walter," Cameko yelled and came after me: "don't do me like this, I like you Walter!"

"I love Yuriko, Cameko, we can never have a serious relationship." Cameko still naked with sex running down her leg came toward me and clung to me. "Help me, Walter!"

"How Cameko?"

"Give me money to go to Mainland, I need to get away from Okinawa."

"Well, won't they follow you?"

"Not if I don't tell them I'm leaving."

"How much do you need?"

"Two thousand dollars."

"I can give it to you Friday." Cameko's faced brightened and she seemed pleased.

"Don't tell anyone Walters, if you do they may try and stop me!"

"I won't tell anyone Cameko I promise." Cameko let me go. I walked out of her sparse apartment smelling like her sex.

Driving back to Base, I realized one thing; that I quickly had become a madman and there was no telling how far this would go. One thing for sure was sex had become my main focus and I didn't want to let go. I only hoped Cameko was serious in trying to escape the Island, Lord knows I didn't plan on giving her money if she had a con going. After I got back to Base, I parked and before I could get inside the Barracks Madison interrupted me. "Everett, we need to talk!"

"Get in the car Madison, it's more private in here." We both got in the car. "Everett about tonight." I cut Madison off:

"You don't need to explain Madison I understand."

"No you don't understand Everett, I'm going on an exercise next week for six months and I wanted to let you know about it." Stunned, I received the news in silence. Now I saw the light, Madison practically threw herself on Thorn perhaps because of sex and now she's telling me she's leaving. "I'll miss you Madison."

"Well Everett I guess you know its official, I'm with Thorn."

"Yes I assumed as much."

"Well aren't you upset?"

"To tell the truth Madison, no, I'm happy for you."

"You mean after all we've been through you're not jealous?"

"Dear child, you have a lot of growing up to do. One day you'll understand my reasoning."

"I see, well is it the Okinawan whore?" Surprised, but nonetheless abreast of the situation I said: "Is that why you didn't want sex Saturday?"

"Thorn told me all about you and some sex tramp called Cameko and I'm certainly not going to get infected by you!"

"Well tell me something Madison how did Thorn know about Cameko if he himself hadn't been with those Oriental whores?"

"His friend Tucker told him some time ago. I didn't believe him at first, but I do now."

"I understand your concern Madison, but I'm perfectly content with my whores." Madison lightly punched me on the arm. "You know I'll miss you Everett, it's been fun, and you certainly are a good lover."

"Why Miss Bilkens that sounds like an invitation."

"No, but if you ever meet me in Lincoln, do call."

"I sure will, now let me give you a ride to the Barracks, it's getting late."

"Sure Mr. Walters whatever you say." I started the engine and prepared to drive Madison back to her barracks. As I turned on the main Street, I went into the opposite direction. "Where on earth are you going?"

"To a motel to screw the hell out of you!" Madison giggled and swore, but didn't protest. I planned on giving her a night to remember despite the scent of Yuriko reeking on me, realizing Madison smelled it. I regretted it being a workday tomorrow, but I had to show Madison who was boss and make her like it.

CHAPTER TEN
RUN CAMEKO

    Tired, sexually drained, but steady, I readied myself for work Thursday. Madison had plenty of spark in her. We didn't leave the Hotel until 0500 hours. Madison at first tried to resist me, but the fight was not in her. She allowed me to undress her and willingly received me. Even though I reeked of Cameko, Madison never mentioned her displeasure. After we made love, Madison told me plenty. I found out she trusted my judgment about Okinawan women. She also confessed that Thorn was a regular of Whisper Alley. I had assumed as much, but I went along with Madison just to play it safe.

    We spoke of my marriage to Yuriko and how I planned to bring her to America one day. Madison wanted to send a gift, but I refused; she had given me plenty. After we left the hotel, I took an exhausted Madison back to her Barracks. I think she lay down with both Thorn and myself. I had slept a bit while with Madison, so I went to the Barracks, showered and prepared for work. I was very thankful when I arrived at work to find that today was vehicle maintenance day. I teamed with Dunbar this morning. "Hey Walters, what's cooking?"

"I really don't know you tell me Dunbar."

"Well I hear Thorns out for a piece of your ass!"

"Oh really?"

"Yeah, he's threatened by you because of Madison. You know Walters if I didn't know any better I think she's trying to play the field."

"You're kidding."

"I'm not certain, but Natalie said that Madison's a confused girl. She also said Madison thinks you're a special guy, but she loves Thorn's way of treating her sexually."

"And how does Thorn treat her?" I demanded.

"Well, Walters, he licks her in places that she's very sensitive about."

"I see. Well Dunbar, you know every man has his limits." Dunbar guffawed so much on that one that he had to go on one knee. Finally he straightened himself. "Now I didn't say you did these things Walters, I'm only telling you the facts."

"I understand Dunbar and thanks for telling me about Thorn, I'll be ready for him."

"Sure Walters, no problem." We began working on our vehicles when Filson walked over and casually observed us. Dunbar noticed him. "What do you say Filson?"

"Not much Dunbar, how are things going over here in the drivers section."

"Just fine couldn't be better Filson." Filson still observed us before saying: "Walters can I speak to you for a minute?"

"Sure Filson." I put my wrench down and stepped over to Filson. When we were out of earshot from Dunbar, Filson spoke: "Look, Walters, I learned from my men that you were at Cameko's last night."

"Yes I was Filson what about it." I asked, snug in my indiscretion with Cameko.

"I'm curious that's it Walters, if you screwed her fine, just don't do drugs with her."

"May I ask why not?"

"Well she's a loose cannon who will spill the beans. I only use her as a go between. Friday I have something for you to deliver to her, be ready." Filson strolled back near the shop. I went back to work. "What are you doing with Filson Walters?"

"Nothing, I just had sex with one of his Okinawan whores that's all."

"That's all, Walters did you know that Filson might be tied up with organized crime?"

"No, I had no idea Dunbar." I wanted to be as ignorant as possible. "You see Walters, right now the Marines won't touch him. From what I hear, top Brass is saying hands off."

"Why so Dunbar?"

"Politics Walters. Filson knows some pretty important people somewhere, enough to back him if he was fingered. How'd you meet him anyway Walters?"

"Let's just say through casual acquaintance."

"Well watch yourself, you never know what lies behind Mr. Filson."

"I will Dunbar." I jumped into the preventive maintenance on the vehicle with my mind dancing with possibilities.

After work I ate chow and headed to the Barracks. I'd do field day and go to the E-Club to try and relax for a while. During field day I was given the assignment of mopping the hallway, which happened to be a huge assignment. It took until 2045 to completely finish the field day, afterwards, I showered, dressed and headed for the Base Club. Tonight happened to be Disco night or the night for Dark Green Marines. I didn't mind being that I liked soul music. I stood at the rear of the Club standing out like a sore thumb. Whites were few and far between, but I'd weather the storm. I started getting some very hostile stares, which I promptly returned, but this was too much! I shrugged it off and went to order a soft drink. Surprisingly, more than a few Marines nodded in my direction as I waded through the sea of dark faces. Right before I made it to the bar, I felt something like an explosion on my right cheek. I lost all sense of myself for a split second then instinctively I realized I had been punched. I whirled in the direction of the hit: it was Thorn; he had cold cocked me and was now waiting for me to react. I didn't want to, but I used my inactive martial arts training. Thorn wasn't expecting a foot. I feinted with my fist and then quickly released a kick on the side of Thorn's face on the temple. Thorn dropped like a bag of rocks. The crowd let out a reserved "ooh." Staff came over and I excused myself. It all happened so quickly I didn't have time to check and see if I was bleeding. I exited the Club and got away as quick as possible. About halfway down the Street, I heard someone calling me. It was Madison. "Everett!" I stopped and turned around. Madison ran toward me with an ankle length purple dress on with high heels. "Everett wait!" Madison caught up with me. "I know you hate me Everett, but I needed to tell you something."

"I don't hate you Madison, it's just that you have immature ways and I'm not sure what you're after right now."

"Everett, Thorn is a nut case. I don't want anything to do with him anymore." Perplexed, I reached for Madison and held her. She started rubbing my wound. "You're bleeding, but just a bit. He socked you quite viciously."

"Yeah, it was a sucker punch, but I understand that's his way."

"Oh, Everett." Madison buried her head in my chest. I held her tightly for a moment inhaling her fragrance. I didn't know what she wanted, but clearing the air was foremost. "Look, Madison, I realize that right now you have mixed feelings. What I don't understand is that you're playing with my emotions as well as Thorn."

"I know Everett, but I never thought he'd attack you."

"Hey, let me walk you to the Barracks Madison, I know you must be really tired by now."

"Yes, I am Everett, thank you." We walked the short distance to the Barracks. When we got there I kissed Madison on the forehead. "Good night Miss Bilkens." Madison smiled and saluted me: "Good night Marine." After she went inside the Barracks I began the long walk to my Barracks.

I made it to the toilet and looked into the mirror. I had a very small cut on my cheekbone, which I didn't bother treating. There was some slight swelling and soreness, so I washed my face and hit the rack. By Friday evening the whole Barracks knew about my actions. They were calling me the white Bruce Lee, which I accepted cheerfully. Thorn, for all credit I gave him turned out to be a country bumpkin. He came over to the Barracks and apologized and swore he'd never touch Madison again. I assured the frightened Thorn that we were all young so don't become so possessive over one female, try dating a few before falling for one you don't know well. Thorn insisted he and Madison were only friends and that I was the one she liked. I patted Thorn on the back and sent him on his way. Not one to laugh at another's shortcomings I at least applauded the young man's courage. He admitted his wrong faced up to me and held his ground. I respected him for that.

That night I had taken three non-drinkers and took them to the package store. I had them all buy two half-gallon bottles of Chivas Regal. It gave me a total of six bottles. I planned on taking them to Mary's. After I took the Marines back to the Barracks, Filson, as usual was waiting for me. "Hey Walters, I have something for you." This time Filson handed me a paper bag that was half full. "Take this to Cameko, Walters, and this time spend the night with her. I don't want anyone getting suspicious you know."

"You think someone knows Filson?"

"Okinawa is only so big Walters, eventually word will get around."

"I see." I took the bag from Filson and put it in my car. After I locked the car I went and got in my stash and took out $2000. I wanted to make sure Cameko got away from Okinawa. With everything put away in the car, I headed to Gate Two Street; however, this night it appeared someone had followed me. I tried to stay calm as though nothing was happening, but I shook like a leaf. Whoever it was stayed at a distance, so I couldn't make out what kind of car it was. I forced myself to stay calm. If I got busted I'd keep a lid on it; I'd take the fall. Very shakily I made it to Cameko's. The car had stopped perhaps a hundred yards down the Street. I took the bag Filson gave me and headed for Cameko's apartment. Quickly getting to the home I knocked on the door, a groggy Cameko opened it. "Walter, you back so soon I thought you come tomorrow."

"Please let me in Cameko, quickly!" Surprised, Cameko stepped aside and let me in.

"What's wrong Walter?"

"Just shut the door and lock it okay." Cameko nonchalantly shut and locked the door. I hadn't realized it but I was sweating profusely. I didn't know what had just happened yet somehow I felt it was tied to Cameko's trip. "Who did you tell about leaving Okinawa Cameko?"

"I never tell anyone but you Walter, why you ask."

"Someone followed me over here." Dammit, I knew I wasn't hallucinating someone actually tailed me, but I'd do as Filson had asked and spend the night here and hopefully things would blow over in the morning. Cameko reminded me: "Walter, you still help me to leave Okinawa okay."

"Yes Cameko, but let's wait here awhile, you can't be too sure about things."

"Okay Walter, we wait here." Cameko went to the small refrigerator and took out two bottles of Bron. She gave me one. "Here Walter, you drink this, it will help calm you down."

"Thanks Yuriko." I opened the bottle and quickly drank it. Curious, I decided to look into the bag Filson gave me. There was dozens of small bags of marijuana and foiled packets. Now I was sure Filson dealt drugs, and he used me to distribute. I closed the bag up and hid it in the refrigerator. "Cameko, how long have you known Filson?"

"For long time Walter, he always have drugs with him."

"Did he have connections with Okinawan gang members?"

"No, someone I don't know told Filson about them and now they work together. They sell drugs to Okinawan people." Now I started piecing things together. Filson probably sold drugs to Americans; he also had Okinawan clientele. The Bastard could get me sent up the River indefinitely. The Bron had begun to take effect. I decided to lie down and let the Bron carry me away. Perhaps 15 minutes later I felt Cameko next to me. Scratching herself, all the while Cameko seemed content. "Walter you sure someone follow you?"

"I'm sure Cameko, someone followed me. You know it's not so much that I'm scared, but I wonder what it is they want."

"Probably the drugs Walter; soon they will knock on the door, then you give them the bag and they will leave; it's okay Walter."

"I hope you're right Cameko." We continued to rest on the bed. I dozed off with trance-like visions. The Bron was some kind of stimulant; I became amazed at its potency.

I must have dozed off because Cameko had left the apartment. I quickly checked the Fridge the bag was gone. Alarmed, I searched the small home, nothing. I heard an exchange of voices outside and froze to intently listen. It was Cameko's voice and it sounded like she had conversations with at least two people. I waited until Cameko came back into the home. She saw that I had awakened. "Walter, why you fall asleep? Two men came by for the bag. They say you see them behind you, but you afraid; they wanted the drugs." I gathered myself trying to pull it together. Whoever it was must have followed me from Base and if so, why? I assumed that question would haunt me for some time. Cameko appeared to get antsy. "Walter, give me the money so I can leave."

"Sure Cameko, we need to go to my car."

"Walter, I'm not coming back here, so take your things."

"So you're really leaving Cameko?"

"I told you Walter, I'm leaving before something happens. Someone is going to get caught and be sent to Japanese Jail." The point drove on me like a sledgehammer. Cameko was absolutely right. This ring would soon come to an end and I wanted to be no part of it. I knew I couldn't run like Cameko, I still happened to be an active duty Marine. I wondered what Chesty Puller would think. I shuddered at the thought.

I watched as Cameko packed two small suitcases. She appeared to be determined to get away. She quickly packed her things then we went outside to my car. I got the money and handed it to Cameko. She took it and put it in the small purse she carried. "Walter, I catch cab okay, I know, they come by every 5 minutes here."

"Okay Cameko." Cameko shoved a piece of paper in my pocket.

"You write me Walter, I will wait for letter from you."

"Sure Cameko I'll write you."

"Bye Walter." Cameko hailed a passing cab.

"Bye Cameko." And just like that she disappeared into the cab. I watched until the cab drove out of sight. I couldn't put my hand on it, but Cameko turned out to be a mysterious person to say the least. I shrugged my shoulder and got into my car. I checked the time 0230 hours. I knew it was very late, so I decided I'd park my car at Mary's and sleep until morning. A bit unnerved I tried to reassess things. I had lost consciousness at Cameko's, so I didn't get to talk to her about her decision to leave Okinawa and why she wanted to leave so abruptly and without her possessions. Getting to Mary's I parked in the small driveway. I shut my car off and let the seat go all the way back, I'd have hell doing it, but I fell into a restless sleep.

I became clear minded at around 0700 hours. The Bron had induced me into a drug like stupor. Whoever it was that followed me didn't come around so maybe Cameko told the truth after all. As I regained my composure I got out of the car and knocked on Mary's door. After several minutes a tired and worn looking Mary answered it. "Walter, come in, you come by early today."

"Yes and I have something for you Mary, some liquor."

"What kind of Liquor Walter?"

"Chivas Regal."

"Good, but I get it later Walter, you come in and get some rest. You tired no?"

"Well yes, I'm a bit tired Mary, but I'll be fine; is Yuriko home?"

"Yes, she still sleeping. You lay on the couch till later until she wakes up."

"Alright Mary anything you say." Mary then took a grab at my crotch. I wrapped my arms around her soft and inviting flesh. Mary giggled before breaking free. "Careful Walter, Yuriko is in love with you, maybe she get mad if she knew we still sleep together."

"Did you tell her that Mary?"

"She knows that you met me at Whisper Alley, but she think we stop having short time."

"I see." Not wanting to disturb Yuriko's young mind, I stopped horsing around with Mary. "Okay Mary I'll get some rest on the couch." Mary quietly smiled and left the room. I put my head down on the couch, apparently more exhausted than I thought because I didn't wake up until three or so hours. Yuriko playfully roused me. "Walter, you need to wake up. You've been sleeping a long time now." An unusually attractive girl, Yuriko had her hair fixed so that it made a ball at the top of her head. It appeared to be in the traditional Japanese style. "I like your hair today Yuriko, it looks nice."

"Thank you Walter, do you want to take a shower this morning?"

"Yes, I think I will Yuriko."

"Okay you go in my room and change and I'll wash your clothes." I dutifully went to Yuriko's small but tidy room and undressed. Naked, I bolted to the restroom and jumped in the small shower. I used whatever I saw in front of me. After thoroughly cleaning myself, I grabbed one of Mary's towels and wrapped it around myself. I went back into Yuriko's room and dried off. As I waited for my clothes to dry, I decided to lie down on Yuriko's bed. Her scent mesmerized me. Dozing off again I fell into a restless sleep. I awakened with Yuriko shaking me, "Walter! Wake up, I need your car keys."

"They are on the table in the sitting room Yuriko."

"Oh, sorry Walter, I didn't notice them there. Anyway my mom wants the liquor to go and sell it."

"It's in the trunk of my car, six bottles of it." I tried to go back to sleep but I couldn't.

"Are my clothes ready yet Yuriko?"

"I need to iron them, they'll be ready in a few minutes." I relaxed and waited for my clothes to dry.

Minutes later Yuriko brought my clothes into the room neatly pressed and folded. "Here you are Walter, now get dressed." Curious, but saying nothing, I wondered why Yuriko didn't come to bed with me. She didn't appear to be upset, so maybe she was waiting on our marriage. Drained, I decided not to pursue sex. I had been a busy person this last week and I could use the rest. I had been so nervous I didn't even think to screw Cameko, which may have been for the best. Today would not have been this pleasant had I smelled of sex and Cameko certainly being a fertile woman, had a strong scent. Maybe that attracted me to her. I dressed and went into the main room. Now it became clear to me Yuriko and her friends sat in the living room waiting for me. "Walter, these are my friends." Yuriko said. Both young girls seemed to size me up before giggling and running out of the house. Perplexed, but pleased, I asked Yuriko: "Is this the custom over here?"

"No my friends just wanted to see if I really had an American boyfriend."

"Now do they believe you?"

"Yes they do. I think they like you Walter, so be careful." Yuriko gave me a naughty look. I smiled and returned the gesture. Yuriko then stood up and came to me. I held her in my arms tightly. "You smell better now Walter." Looking around for Mary I ignored Yuriko's last statement and asked: "Where's Mary?"

"She took my little sister to go and sell the liquor you brought over."

"Oh, and what do you plan on doing young lady?" Yuriko let her hair down and walked toward her bedroom. I, despite myself, thanked the stars I had put Cameko's address in my glove box. Lord knows the hell that would have taken place had Yuriko found it. Erect and steady I forgot about being sexually drained. This young feline had charged me up just by unbuttoning her blouse.

CHAPTER ELEVEN
LOVE HURTS

Marriage to Yuriko turned out to be my most pleasurable decision I had ever made besides joining the Corps. We had been married over two months. The February air tickled me now that I had my soul mate. I had moved in with Mary a month ago. I couldn't get enough of my exotic flower. Mary, for the most part, did the cooking, cleaning and budgeting. Yuriko finishing up school continually attended and I had my commitment to the Corps. Madison had long gone and surprisingly she never wrote. I had given her my address and she promised she would. I figured she found another lover and went about her usual business. Moving off Base, I still had to contend with Filson, who was as diabolical as could be. Filson moved another Okinawan woman into Cameko's old apartment. He didn't appear to upset about Cameko, and I wasn't telling him anything.

Filson now gave me packets at work when he felt sure no one paid attention to us. I'd put it in my trunk and deliver it to Hadeki, who now resided at Cameko's. It irritated me to still have to deal with Filson, but I had no choice. I was cornered with only my submission as safety. After formation on a beautiful Friday morning, I was called into Lieutenant Wikenburg's office. "Lance Corporal Walters, how does it feel to be promoted?"

"Good, sir, I can't wait to become Corporal in the U.S. Marine Corps."

"That may happen sooner than you think son." Curious, but not questioning the C.O., he asked me to sit down. "Look, Walters, you are going T.A.D. next week, so I want you to have all your shit ready to go."

"Sir, I just got married for Christ' sake."

"I know son, but believe me you'll like it."

"I don't understand sir?"

"We need good Marines like you to represent H & S Company Walters, now I know you'll make us proud Marine. But I'm giving you today and all of next week to prepare, you're leaving by flight Friday next week." Stunned, I sat in the C.O.'s office. I couldn't believe this. Temporary duty was one thing, but leaving Yuriko would be devastating. I wanted to tell the C.O. to screw himself, but I had no choice, the Lieutenant had given me the order. "As you were Marine!" I quickly popped out of my thoughts: "Yes Sir!"

"Go to Headquarters and get your orders son, you have a couple of days to get ready, so get to it Marine!"

"Aye Aye, Sir." I left the office befuddled and unsure of myself. I had learned that the Corps could pull the rug right out from under you, but even for the Corps this was ridiculous. Nonetheless, I followed orders and went to get my assignment papers. Packing would not be a problem; I could do that in a couple of hours. What I needed to do was plan a way for Yuriko to come with me.

As I went to get my orders, I tried to mentally prepare a way to fly my new family with me. After going to Administration and picking up my orders I saw that I'd be heading to Mainland Japan to Camp Fuji. To my surprise, Dunbar had orders to go there too. Apparently at the last minute we both were volunteers by Wikenburg. I at least had company now. I picked up my orders and then I had Dunbar ride with me to the Package Store and pick up some Liquor. Mary still sold items I picked up at the exchange and now Yuriko had access to the exchange being that she had a dependents I.D. card.

Before I got home to tell everyone the news, I braced myself, but first I had a package to deliver to Hadeki. Filson had been giving me quite a number of packages lately it had become alarming. When I arrived at the apartment, I knocked on the door several times before a young woman probably in her twenties opened the door. "Is Hadeki here?"

"No, she is with her family, what do you need, I can help." The young lady had the typical Oriental accent. "Well, I need to put this package in the Fridge, is that okay?"

"Yes, she say American come to give her packet it's okay."

"Thank you." I walked over to deliver the package. The young lady followed me: "What's your name, I don't think we've met."

"You can call me Sally."

"Sure, I'm Walters." Sally stuck out her hand and I shook it. "So what do you do for work Sally?"

"I'm a Bar girl I work at night."

"So do you have a boyfriend, Sally?"

"I have a lot of boyfriends, you want short time Walters?"

"How much Sally."

"Give me $50 and you stay long time." Not wanting to commit adultery, but wanting to stick it to Filson as much as I could, I finished around in my wallet until I counted $50. "Here you are Sally right on the spot." Sally took the money and put it on a dresser.

"You come to the bedroom okay." I quietly followed Sally to the bedroom. She wore a pink night robe, which she promptly stepped out of. "Whew, Sally, look at you." Sally had an exquisite figure, not as pretty as Yuriko, but she had curves. I, as usual, sprang to attention. I got out of my camouflage utilities as quickly as I could and stood there naked and ready. Sally, for all of her forwardness acted rather inexperienced. I walked over to her and embraced her and she tightened up. "Relax Sally, I won't hurt you." I tried to lay her on the bed. She refused at first, but she finally gave in and lay down. Realizing she was nothing but a young girl didn't deter me from carnal lust. "Take it easy Sally, I just want to like you." I climbed on top of the young vixen. I kept trying to enter her, but I couldn't. Finally, out of frustration I said: "You put it in Sally."

"Okay, but take it easy I still dry."

"I will Sally." She guided me in, yes; she was certainly dry and inexperienced. "I thought you had many boyfriends." I said just as that overwhelming feelings of sex begin to take over.

Taking it easy at first I felt Sally lubricating. Desire taking over I went in motion. My ejaculation came in spurts. Not the regular explosion that I was accustomed to. I decided to get up quickly. I figured Sally was Hadeki's little sister who wanted to make a quick buck. I didn't want to be caught here with Sally, so I dressed quickly and left. Not saying a word to Sally who still lie on the bed staring at the ceiling. When I arrived at Mary's, I opened the door to an empty house. I went and quickly showered and changed clothes.

I awakened to Mary carefully nudging me. "Walter, why you home so soon?"

"I have bad news Mary, I'm being shipped off to Mainland next week."

"Mainland!" Mary covered her mouth in disbelief.

"Yeah, I feel the same way Mary, I was told this morning at the Motor Pool."

"How long will you stay Walter?"

"I'm not sure Mary its temporary duty." Both Mary and I remained silent. I could see the hurt in Mary's eyes. Yuriko and I really hit it off, we had begin to be a family. I wrote my grandmother sparingly, but I had never told her of my new family here in the Orient. I wanted to surprise her. "Walter, you tell Yuriko when she first come home, don't wait."

"I will Mary the minute she gets here." Mary left the room before I could tell her about the liquor in my car. Maybe now wasn't a good time for that anyway.

I slept several hours before hunger had awakened me. I got up to get a snack. Yuriko, who must have come home sooner than I expected, was preparing something that smelled real good. "What are you cooking dear?"

"I'm cooking beef stew. My mom and I decided to give you a good old fashioned American dish." I went and stood behind my new bride.

"I'm so happy we are married Yuriko, I never realized you'd turn out to be such a loving girl." Yuriko looked over her shoulder and added: "I like you too Walters." I let her get back to her cooking. I'd tell her about my move after dinner, why spoil such a tasty meal. After Kim came home from school, I never talked to Kim much and she seemed to like that even better. Coming of age, Kim had started sprouting breast and her hips began to spread. Ignoring my senses, I sat down with the family to eat dinner. As we bowed our heads, I realized that I hadn't actually experienced an Okinawan bowing which was their customary greeting. After we all said our silent prayers, I dug into my meal. Excellent; the stew had plenty of beef to go along with the vegetables. I had several helpings before excusing myself. "Excuse me everyone I have some things I need to do." Yuriko stood up and went with me.

Once we got in the bedroom, I decided to tell her the news. "Look, Yuriko, I'm going to have to go to Mainland Japan for at least six months; temporarily." Yuriko buried her face in her hands. "Why are they sending you away so soon Walters?"

"That's the Marine Corps way sweetheart. We're on call 24 hours a day." Yuriko reached for me. I held her tightly as I thought of a plan to keep us together. Yuriko, a strong girl silently cried on my shoulder.

That night while we both lay in bed, I came up with a solution that might work. I'd send for Yuriko after I had gotten established on the Mainland and we'd rent an apartment together. I checked the time; it was almost midnight. I quietly got out of bed and got dressed. I put on my casual polo shirt and jeans. Ever so quiet, so as not to disturb Yuriko, I left the room. With my identification and my car keys, I softly exited the home. I put the liquor in the home just in case. I pushed my car out to the driveway and down the street. Yards away I started my car and headed for Gate Two Street. Once there I parked my car. Being that payday was a few days ago; the streets were teeming with Americans. I decided to go to one of the Rock n Roll joints to check and see if I could locate anyone from Base that I could associate with.

When I went inside the Club I didn't see anyone that I knew. I went inside anyway; the music blared as I tried to find a seat. The place overflowed with veterans and Bargirls. I turned to leave and a hand grabbed my elbow; it was Natalie from Base. "Keep walking." Natalie said. We got outside away from the music. "Hello Natalie how are you?"

"I'm fine Mr. Walters." We both looked straight ahead as we walked. "Walters, you don't seem surprised to see me here."

"To be honest Natalie I'm not. I've learned to expect anything on the Island." Natalie giggled and continued walking with me. Not a bad looking woman after all. Natalie had a rather slim figure, which went well with her short-cropped blonde hair. A short girl, she had an excellent complexion, but she did have an unusual gap in her front teeth. Almost masculine in appearance, but she handled it well. "Walters with the rumors swirling around base about you I'm not surprised by your last statement."

"What did you hear Natalie?"

"Plenty; Madison wasn't one to hold her tongue you know." Curious I broke the conversation. "What brings you out tonight Natalie, I figured you'd be with Dunbar to say the least."

"Dunbar is what you say an introvert when it comes to being social. He likes to stay on the base. You know I believe he's timid of the locals. I'm actually out here with another male friend, but he is so wasted he didn't even react when I stopped you. I'm glad you came into the Bar Walters, you spared me the horror of a bunch of drunken servicemen plying for my attention."

"What are you going to do now Natalie?"

"First, I'll tell you the scoop. Did you know that Miss Madison is pregnant."

"No I didn't, I'm shocked to hear that."

"You were the last Marine to have her before she left, she's sure of it."

"Where's she now Natalie?"

"They sent her back to America Walters. Camp Lejune." I whistled at the revelation.

"What else did you hear Natalie?"

"That you are a big-time hustler with some heavy people."

"I see, where did you hear that?"

"From Dunbar, he's always fishing for dirt on someone."

"Well, I'm sorry to disappoint you Natalie, but I'm no hustler." Natalie smiled and continued walking with me. "Where are you headed now Natalie?"

"Probably to Lido's, I know a dark Green W.M. that came out here with me. I'll stick around and see if she's still there."

"Mind if I tag along?"

"Not a problem Walters." We continued walking until we passed Whisper Alley. I was not sure if Mary worked this late, so I walked as quickly as possible past the Street. It was still fairly busy out here. Natalie giggled as we went by Gate Two. "I bet you have had your fill here, huh, Walters.'

"To say the least Natalie, you know it has its place." Natalie punched me on the shoulder. "Why would anyone want it that way?"

"You have to remember Natalie is that this is not America, this is Okinawa, remember that."

"So you're saying that guys can't get a regular girlfriend?"

"No, I'm saying that there isn't a lot of girls to go around Natalie."

"Well, in my opinion they should wait until they get home then." I let the remark sink in. Natalie had a point, but only a deeply religious man would wait until he got off the Island to have relations.

As we walked into the Night Club, the soul music greeted us. Not at its peak, nonetheless, Lidos' had good business. "Thanks for walking me over Walters." Then Natalie dispersed in the crowd before I could reply. Alone I looked around to see if I could identify anyone. When I didn't I decided to exit the hole in the wall. I wasn't sure, but I could have sworn I saw Filson sitting at the Bar with Sally. That helped my decision to depart Lidos.

I quickly darted from Lidos and Gate Two and went to my car and headed back to Mary's. When I got back into the bedroom, Yuriko lie in bed waiting. I felt grateful that I had not had sex because sure enough, Yuriko sniffed me. "Where did you go Walters?" She asked still sleepy. "I had to go think about you coming with me to Mainland. I want you to come with me Yuriko."

"I don't know Walters, I'm scared of going to Mainland. It's not like Okinawa, a lot can happen there."

"Yuriko if you stay in Okinawa something might happen."

"I don't understand Walters." It gnawed me to the bone not to tell Yuriko of my dealings with organized crime, but she never would understand my position. "You sure you want to stay here Yuriko?"

"No, I'm not sure, but this is where I want us to stay. I don't want you to leave Walters." Yuriko turned in the bed facing away from me. I cuddled next to her and tried to comfort her. Exhausted, I soon lost consciousness.

I awakened to the sound of Yuriko talking to Mary. They seemed to be discussing something that concerned me. "Hello you two, what's going on?" Mary spoke first.

"Walter, we talk of Yuriko going to Mainland. You send for her?"

"Yes I will Mary as soon as I can." Mary didn't appear convinced.

"Walter, did you want to go to Mainland or they ask you?"

"NO it wasn't my idea Mary, my company sent me." Mary must have thought I wanted to go to Mainland to screw as many women as possible, but I couldn't accept that assumption in front of Yuriko. Yuriko kissed me on the cheek. "I'm going to get breakfast ready."

"Okay Yuriko, I'll shower and then I'll come in the sitting room." Yuriko put on her robe and both she and Mary left the room for the kitchen. I understood Mary's logic, I had exhibited some freakish behavior to her and now she figured I wanted to sow some wild oats. Anyway I couldn't stop thinking of Natalie early this morning telling me that Madison possibly carried my child. It wouldn't leave my mind, a baby, damn! I got out of bed and headed for the shower.

The rest of the weekend went without incident. I had packed my military gear and Monday I'd get my 782 gear. Everything had to be packed for mobility and I expected the Corps to fly us over since both

Dunbar and I were notified after the Company had already shipped out. As Monday morning rolled around I prepared to go to Base. I drove to the Base leaving Yuriko, who had planned to go to school; Mary still slept; not wanting to disturb Mary I quietly departed the home. At work, Dunbar and I were excused to check out. "Come on Dunbar, we can ride in my car it will go faster."

"Great, thanks Walters." We took out time walking the short distance to my car. "Hey what did you do this weekend Dunbar?"

"I stayed on Base Walters, I don't know about you, but I like my weekends to sleep in."

"So did you spend anytime with Natalie?"

"No, but she told me about the conversation she had with you. Thanks for bailing her out of that Club."

"Why, what did she tell you?"

"She said you rescued her from a rather bad environment."

"It was nothing, I believe she spotted me first."

"Oh, really?" Dunbar asked amused. I nodded my head extinguishing any sort of fireworks. We jumped into my car and headed to the Company Barracks we'd begin check out there. After two hours we had completed the check out. Now we needed to get our gear out of Supply. Dunbar didn't ask me any more questions regarding Natalie during check out, but now he started again. "Tell me something Walters, you being married now how do you manage to still hang out on Gate Two Street?"

"Energy Dunbar, I have plenty of it to expend."

"Did you try anything with Natalie?" Surprised, but not offended I said: "You know Dunbar if you got out more, you'd be more secure about Natalie."

"It's not that Walters, I don't mind Natalie's indiscretions, as a matter of fact, we don't screw that much, we have a platonic sort of relationship you know."

"Oh really, then why did you want to know if I made a pass at her?"

"To tell the truth Walters, you do have a reputation of being a stud courtesy of Madison Bilkens, and Natalie's a woman if you hadn't noticed Walters."

"Still, Dunbar, Natalie and I talked of Madison's status and little or nothing about anything else. Sex wasn't part of the conversation." Dunbar grunted as we parked and went toward supply. "Anyway Walters, since I'm going on this exercise she's fair game."

"You mean you're not going to keep her?"

"Naw, Natalie's a free spirit, I'm more of an old-fashioned person let her roam if that's what she wants." I didn't comment about Lidos', Dunbar didn't bring it up and I wasn't asking. We received out gear and went back to my car. "Dunbar, I'm hungry, I'm going to get a bite to eat at the Snack Bar, you game?"

'Sure, I need something for my thirst." We headed for the Base Snack Bar.

After snacking I took Dunbar to the Barracks to drop off his gear. Being finished for the day, I started toward my car when Filson interrupted me. "Hey Walters, hold on a second." I stopped and turned around. Filson had an over night bag he carried on his shoulders. "I need a ride to work Walters."

"Hop in Filson." We headed toward the Motor Pool. Filson put the overnight bag in the back seat. "Walters, I want you to take this bag to Camp Foster, to a Marine that will meet you at the reception center. He knows who you are, so just park and he'll come and get the bag." Filson took out a thick envelope and stuck it under my seat. "A little something for America's hero, and have a fun exercise, I'll miss you."

"I'll miss you too Filson!"

"Like hell you will." Filson burst into laughter. A strange man, Fislon, whatever drove him never seemed afraid or agitated. A calculated man who appeared to know which screws to turn. As we approached the Motor Pool, but before we could be notice by anyone, Filson blurted out; "stop right here Walters!"

"Sure Filson, no problem." I stopped and let the nimble marine out of my car. Filson said nothing as he shut the door. I continued on my way to Camp Foster. Thinking on the way over, I wondered exactly what the contents happened to be in the bag. Possibly drugs, but it could have been something else. Perhaps money, I didn't want to check it only I wanted to get rid of it and continue with my matters.

As I arrived at Camp Foster I again became nervous. The Gate Guard passed me through and I zipped passed him. Remembering reception I drove their as safe as the situation allowed. When I got there a Marine was there waiting. He stared as I drove in the reception parking lot. He motioned toward me letting me know he knew who I was. I parked, took the bag out of the car and walked toward him. "Walters?" I nodded my head in agreement. He reached for the bag and I gave it to him. He accepted it and quickly handed me a rolled wad of cash. Surprisingly at this hour very few people circulated around reception. He didn't give me his name and I refused to ask. I watched the medium build Marine as he turned and headed back to the Barracks. He wore Sergeant Stripes, which amazed me. A black Marine, but he carried himself as having authority and power. Unusual to say the least, I could reason maybe a Drill Instructor at one point in his Marine Corps career. Not an old man, but he did look mature. I admired his aura. I put the wad of cash in my pocket and nervously went back to my car. Thinking of Mary, I decided to go shopping at the Base Exchange. I knew what Mary liked, so there wasn't a problem getting the items she'd sell. Forcing myself to do it I purchased over $100 worth of groceries. I quickly took the items to my car and loaded them in. I had purposely purchased items for Hadeki and Sally. I wanted to show my respect. I checked the time; it was 1235 hours. Driving to Cameko's old apartment I thought about her. I didn't write her yet, but I never forgot my first love. Ironically Cameko knew Filson the whole time I knew her. She appeared so innocent I never dreamed she was involved with criminals. If it hadn't have been for meeting Mary, I'd still believe Cameko's words that I was different and she liked me. How naïve I must have been! Tucker as it turned out was a small-time person. He had no clue about Cameko's actual dealings, or like Tucker warned me prior about Yakuza, he refused to play the game. Either way I was involved up to the neck and the worst part about it, I rather enjoyed the activity. Now that I had to leave the Island, I wondered if Yuriko and I would stay together. I truly hoped that we could.

I arrived at Cameko's place. Still early Sally no doubt still stayed home at this time of the day. I took some items with me as I went to knock on the door. After a few knocks a sleepy looking Sally opened the door. I had surprised her. "What you want?" She asked eying the bag of groceries. I stuck out the groceries. "These are for you Sally."

"Thank you." She said and took the bag. I invited myself in and took a seat. The place still had not been decorated; they must have been concerned only with exchanging sex for money here. After Sally put the groceries away, she came and sit down next to me. "I forget your name."

"You can call me Walter."

"Okay, Walter."

"Yes?'

"You want short time now. I'm okay now, I won't be dry this time."

"Yes, but, tell me something Sally, do you know a person called Filson here on the Island?"

"I do, he's my friend's boyfriend."

"Hadeki?"

"Yes."

"Where is she now Sally?"

"At work, she work all day."

"Where does she work Sally?" Sally giggled and stood up.

"She work at Japanese Bar."

"I see; where do you work Sally?"

"I don't have job, I'm Bar girl." I put my arm around Sally and squeezed her. I knew she had little experience at what she was doing, she tried to appear tough, but she didn't fool me. I wanted to question her about Filson, but that would indeed be dangerous. Heaven knows that I still had to think of Yuriko and my safety. I looked Sally in the eyes: "Sally, you take groceries and use them, but don't tell anyone who their from okay?"

"Okay Walter, I won't." Sally embraced me and whispered in my ear. "Let's do short time Walter." I knew I had time, but marriage made me a little more sensitive. I showed Sally my ring. "I love my girl Sally, yes I'd like short time, but not right now. I wanted to give you the groceries for last time." Sally appeared to be perplexed, but regained her composure. She laughed before saying: "I remember you leave too soon Walter, I still want to make love to you. Why did you leave?"

"I thought someone was coming, so I left to avoid trouble." Sally nodded her head. I wasn't sure if she understood or not, buy I didn't repeat myself. "Look, Sally, I have to get going okay."

"We make love for you okay?" Not really wanting to have the smell of sex on me, but Sally happened to be an attractive girl. The urges got the better of me. I stood and pulled Sally to her feet. I embraced her grabbing her shapely bottom in the process. "You win Sally." I stepped back and began undressing Sally. She didn't protest, but helped me do the job. "This time I won't get scared Walter."

"Why were you scared before Sally?"

"I don't know you, so I'm nervous, but not now."

"Good." I undressed and left my clothes at my feet. My erection at its peak caught Sally's attention. I wanted to go to bed, but I thought I'd try something different. I picked Sally up and tried to enter her standing up. She was heavier than I thought. Forget this! So I sat her back on the ground. "Let's go to the bedroom Sally." Sally silently led me to the bedroom. We both got under the covers and embraced. Sally giggled and squirmed to my touch. If she was a pro, she sure didn't act like it. Excited and horny now, I turned Sally over on her back and quickly entered her. She was ready for me this time. I began the session feeling as guilty as ever.

This time when we finished I stuck around for a bit. I showered well and put on some of the cologne that was in the rest room. Sally, as it turned out happened to be a very friendly girl. I knew I screwed her only to spite Filson, but I had a good time in the process. After 2 or more hours with Sally, I left and headed to Mary's. I had everything necessary to go to Mainland. My orders stated that I was to report to Kadena Air Base Friday at 0600 hours. I'd be prepared to leave and get there early, so I didn't run into problems that might delay me or cause me to miss the flight; I decided to call Jonah Crockett and let him keep the Datsun for me. I knew Mary would have no use for it. Yuriko may have wanted to learn to drive, but she didn't want standard shift.

When I arrived at Mary's there was no one home. I took everything out of the car and brought it into the home. I neatly packed my 782 gear and set it with my uniforms and cargo. Tomorrow I'd have to put a lot of my belongings in Supply. Wanting a nap I finally was able to lie down. A million thought roared through my mind as I contemplated the future. I wondered what exactly waited for me in Mainland.

CHAPTER TWELVE
CHECKING OUT

Thursday, I awakened feeling as though I had lost my way. Yuriko had gotten mad at me last night and decided to sleep in Kim's bedroom. Flustered I tried to join them, but it frightened young Kim. I tried to explain to Yuriko that there was nothing I could do about going to Mainland and that I'd try to send for her. I wasn't sure how I'd travel during those next six months. I didn't want to leave Yuriko for any extended period of time while I trained. Being the young girl that she is, Yuriko had been adamant that I wanted to sleep with scores of women and have a jolly good time. She didn't understand that I loved her and other women would not be on the agenda. As Yuriko stormed out of the room, I watched in amazement and wondered; what the hell was Cameko saying when she stated that 'Oriental girl is different from American; if anything, they're more sensitive to cheating. I grimaced thinking of how Yuriko's feelings had turned if she knew about my discretions.

I dressed and grabbed a fruit for breakfast; I jumped in my car and headed for Base. With everything taken care of I wanted to make sure I left nothing out. Eating the fruit on the way I contemplated things. I wanted to catch Jonah at home, but I'd have to wait until the evening. I knew he'd be at work all day. As early as it showed on my watch, I didn't know where to go. I knew going to the Motor Pool in my civilian clothing was a no-no. Wikenburg certainly wouldn't allow that. I decided to drive to Naha and entertain myself for a while, maybe see if there happened to be something I might get into. I rarely came to these parts, I knew Naha to be a bustling part of Okinawa, but I had become so accustomed to Gate Two Street activities that Naha looked like it was for amateurs.

Naha, busy this morning, but not overcrowded, I found a spot to park my car and I ventured out to see the city. A clean and well-kept place, there were so many shops and stores here. It's amazing to see the native ply their wares. I walked around noticing everything. Being so early in the day didn't give me time to do much. As I browsed I spotted a small and inviting Bar still open. I walked over and glance inside and to my delight only several customers stayed inside. I ducked in and took a seat in the corner. The place was dark and bare, with maybe 5 tables and a Bar. The Oriental music still played softly. Not a lot of decorations just enough to keep one curious. What stood out on the wall happened to be a large picture of a Japanese woman who appeared to be very prominent. As I took my seat, an older Okinawan woman came over, "May I help you?"

"Yes, let me have a Seven Up please." The woman smiled, apparently grateful that I didn't order a drink at this hour.

She walked back over to the Bar, and seconds later she arrived with a Coke. "We have no more Seven Up. Sorry."

"That's fine, I'll take the Coke Nason." Pleased she put the Coke on the table. "$3 please." Working hard to keep my composure I went to my wallet. I had almost forgotten that I had the wad of cash I had put in it from my dealings with Filson's associate. I gave her a $10 bill. She gave me change and walked away. Trying to get along with the music I slowly drank my soda. Out of nowhere a middle-aged woman came out and sat down beside me. "Hi, I'm Omi." I stuck out my hand:

"I'm Walters, nice to meet you." She invited herself to sit down. "You know Walters, it's not often we see Americans at this time of day." Impressed by her English skills, I took note. "To tell the truth, Omi, I'm just passing time here."

"I see, well would you like some company?"

"Sure." Omi raised her hand and the older woman quickly came over. Omi ordered a scotch. I assumed I was paying so I said: "So tell me something Omi, where did you learn such good English?" I mentioned as I paid for the drink. Pleased that I had been so observant Omi replied. I went to Tokyo University for two years. There I learned English well." Picking up on my surprise Omi continued: "Oh, don't worry, this isn't my only job, but this is my Bar." Omi saw she had my attention. "Yes, Walters, sometimes I get lonely too."

"You're an attractive woman Omi, I don't understand."

"You see, Walters, I travel a lot, so I come here to relax and catch my breath, usually Americans don't come here because of the hours we keep. We're an after-hours Bar."

"I wouldn't be here Omi, but I'm leaving the Island soon and I had some spare time, so I thought I'd check out Naha and sight see." Omi noticed my ring. "I see you're married."

"Yes, to a lovely Okinawan her name is Yuriko."

"That's such a pretty name, do you have kids?"

"No, we're just married." Omi took a sip of her drink.

"I never married myself, never had the time."

"So tell me Omi, why didn't you stay at the University?"

"I went to Europe and finished my studies. Then I spent a little time in China before I settled here on Okinawa."

"Are you from Okinawa Omi?"

"No, I am originally from San Francisco." I had to refrain my surprise, but couldn't.

"America!" Omi laughed and threw her head back.

"Yes, I lived there for six years with my parents. They were immigrants. They settled in Mainland though, they said America is too dangerous, to many guns." I nodded my head in agreement. "Hey Walters, I have a place near here, and I'm tired, why don't you come back some other time and we'll talk." Trying to capitalize on the situation I said: "I'm free today, maybe I can come too." Omi smiled and reminded me, "But you're married."

"Omi, it's been a while since I've talked with a mature person. I'd really enjoy talking to you more." Omi thought about it then she said: "Well, you do seem to be a pleasant person, how about we talk on the way over, you walk me home."

"I have a car Omi, if I can find it."

"That's nice Walters, you owning a vehicle here on Okinawa, but I don't live very far."

"Well, I'll find it again wherever it's parked, but I'd love to walk you home."

"Just a minute Walters, I'll be right back, I have to let my workers know to close shop."

"Okay Omi." After Omi went to the Bar, I checked the time, not even 0900 hours. I had left home quite early. I hated to have Yuriko upset at me like this. She really took it hard no doubt Mary had some input on this, but I'd try to straighten everything out when I got home. Omi quickly came back with her purse. "You ready Walters?"

"I'm ready Omi." As we left the Bar, I checked Omi out. Not bad probably 35 to 40, a bit chubby but cute. Raven black hair and chubby cheeks. Omi had the potential to attract just about any man. Omi noticed me observing her: "You like what you see Walters?"

"Very much so Omi." She laughed and slipped her arm around mine. "You're very handsome yourself Walters." We both smiled at each other and continued walking. After walking some 15 minutes through the heart of the city, oblivious of onlookers we came up on some high-rise apartments, at least for Okinawa. "You see Walters, I don't live very far from my Bar."

"So tell me Omi, why don't you settle down and get married?"

"I did once and it didn't work out."

"How long were you married?"

"Oh, about 2 years; I was young and didn't know what I wanted and he was an older man. I thought he'd mature but he didn't. We divorced and he gave me money and that was that."

"Do you mind me asking how old you are Omi?"

"No, not at all, I'm 35 years old Walters, am I too old for you?" Omi looked flirtingly at me and smiled. "No, you're just right Omi." As we went into the complex our arms still linked, Omi tightened her grip. Rather tall for an Okinawan, Omi walked me over to an elevator. "I live on the top floor, I have a nice view of the Ocean from my apartment."

"These are nice apartments Omi."

"Thank you, Walters." We got in the elevator and rode until we arrived at the top floor. I didn't try anything with Omi, fearing she may not accept my advances. As we departed the elevator Omi turned to me and said: "I've never invited an American to my home before Walters."

"Why not Omi?" I asked curiously.

"Because I rarely get to meet them the way you and I met. Most of the time I bring older Oriental men here." We walked down the semi large complex until Omi stopped at a door at the end of the building. "I live right here Walters." I waited while Omi opened the door; as we went inside I could see that Omi had taste. The apartment, medium size had off white walls with beige carpet. Omi had a small living room with two love seats facing a big screen television. "Don't forget to take off your shoes Walters." I took off my adidas sneakers and walked over to one of the love seats. "Would you like a drink, Walters?"

"No, I'm fine Omi."

"Well, I could use one myself." Omi went to a small Bar near the front entrance and fixed a drink. I enjoyed the view of the Ocean out of the large window: "You're right Omi, that is a nice view."

"See, I really enjoy looking out of it to relieve stress sometimes." Omi came over and sat down and invited me to do the same. "Have a seat, Walters." I took a seat and made myself comfortable. Omi took a sip of her drink. "You know Walters, I really feel good about you. You seem like such a nice guy. I had no fear about bringing you here."

"Are you lonely Omi?" I asked reaching at straws hoping to arouse Omi's desire.

"Well to be honest Walters, no I'm not, I only wanted to continue our conversation, but now I feel okay." I sensed Omi wanted to relax:

"Omi, if you're wanting to get some sleep I understand."

"Would you like to come too, but only sleep, no fooling around okay." Disappointed, but happy I had a place to kill time I agreed. When we went into the bedroom, I looked around impressed at what I saw. Omi had really decorated the small room. A double bed in the center of the room, highlighted by a matching set of what appeared to be Oak furniture. Omi also had a full-length mirror that sat between the dresser and closet.

I waited for Omi to lie down. A bit shocked when she began to undress, I watched with enthusiasm. Omi felt right at home undressing in front of me and got in bed under the covers. She had one would say a lovable figure. Plump but appealing, despite myself, I found that feeling of desire coming to life inside of me. I lay down fully dressed on top of the covers. "Oh, no, Walters, you need to be comfortable, so get undressed and get under the blanket."

"As you wish Omi." I gladly replied to the scantily dressed woman. I snuggled next to Omi and as I felt her warmth, I really became excited. "Oh, you're a bad boy Walters, he, he." With that clue I wrapped my arms around Omi as she lay on her side. She didn't protest, but she never reached for me. Exhausted from arguing with Yuriko, I felt the sleep coming on. Even though I wanted to have sex with Omi I lost consciousness before I knew it.

I awakened several hours later to an empty bed. I checked the time; it read 1345 hours. I decided to stay in bed and wait for Omi to return. I became relieved when she came back in the room. "I had to use the toilet, Walters." I observed Omi in her panties and bra, she really turned me on, but I wanted her to make the first move. Omi climbed in bed. "You're a naughty boy Walters, you really were trying to have sex with me earlier."

"In my sleep?" I asked incredulously.

"Yes, in your sleep young man!" Omi giggled and turned in bed facing me. "So, what are your plans with your wife Walters?"

"To tell the truth Omi, I really love Yuriko and I plan on staying with her forever if possible."

"Do you plan on taking her back home with you?"

"Why of course, I feel strongly about it. Why wouldn't I do that, she's my wife for Pete's sake!"

"It's not that I am concerned about it, it's family."

"What do you mean Omi?'

"They may not except her because of her nationality and the problem both of our countries have had with each other."

"I see." I hadn't given that much thought, but there was no way my family would reject Yuriko especially now that she's part of the family. No, Omi was wrong on this one. "You know Omi, I don't think my family is like that really;" Omi gave me a concerned look, but she didn't reply. Surprisingly, she began caressing my hair. "You are such a handsome man Walters, I bet you didn't have problems getting an American girl, no?"

"I tried to wait until I found the right girl Omi, one that I really admired and respected. Sure, they're scores of women in the States, but I guess being picky didn't help matters much."

"Do you have girlfriends in the States Walters?"

"I had friends Omi, but nothing like I found over here."

"You mean your wife of Okinawa."

"Both." Omi smiled again and continued to caress me. Now she moved to my chest. "Do you work out Walters?"

"On occasion Omi, why do you ask me that." I playfully asked getting into the act by rubbing Omi on her butt, my hand touching the silky-smooth panties. I must have hit the spot for what began as playful rubbing now turned into frantic lustful grabs. I didn't realize touching Omi in those sensitive areas would cause her to respond so hungrily. Omi moved in close to me, skin to skin. We started some light kissing at first and then some heavy tongue dancing. I tasted all the fish favor of Omi and it was pleasant. Omi began to moan with pleasure and reaching for me again. I obliged and we quickly took off the remainder of my clothing.

After the sex I held Omi next to me. She was the first to speak after catching her breath. "I feel terrible for doing this Walters, I shouldn't have let things get this far."

"don't do that to yourself Omi, it's natural for a man and woman to desire each other, especially being this close together."

"Maybe you're right Walters, besides, Okinawan girl knows that her husband is going to have girlfriends besides his wife."

"I've heard that before Omi, is that the custom here in Okinawa?"

"For Okinawans it is, but Americans may be viewed differently."

"So, you're saying if I was Okinawan, Yuriko would give me problems?"

"Probably not she would understand the culture." I remained silent caressing Omi in the process. She enjoyed being intimate with me. It appeared she hadn't been with a man in some time. We both drifted back to sleep. I woke up to Omi calling my name: "Walters, wake up, it's time to go!" I sat up in bed and checked the time. It was well past 1700 hours. Where did the time go? I got out of bed and asked Omi could I shower. She knowingly smiled and guided me to the small well-kept rest room.

I took a thorough shower completely washing the sex from me. I didn't want Yuriko to have more reasons to be mad at me. After showering I quickly dressed. Omi waited for me. "Will you walk me back to my Club Walters?"

"Sure Omi, no problem." Omi didn't say anything, which let me know that she didn't expect to sleep with me. Emotions got out of hand. She certainly wasn't selling herself and I didn't want to spoil the moment by asking about a price. As we left the apartment, Omi gave me a long kiss. "Thank you Walters, that was nice." I smiled a long wide smile and embraced Omi.

"Thank you for being so nice Omi." Arm in arm we headed for the Bar. When we got there, I thanked Omi for the good time again. She told me to keep quiet as she quickly went in the Bar. She smiled, but ignored me. Taking the signal I hurriedly walked away from the Bar. When I got back to my car it was after 1800 hours. I drove toward Jonah's as fast as possible. I ran to the door hoping to catch Jonah at home. After several knocks, a stern Jonah opened it. At first, he wanted to yell, but he realized it was I. "Hey Walters, what's up?"

"Jonah, I came over to ask you to keep my car for me while I go over to Mainland." Surprised, Jonah gave me a funny look. "You mean you've been on the Island this long and you're just telling me Walters?"

"Jonah, it's a very long and sad story, you'd never understand."

"I have nothing but time Walters, come in."

"What about Monique?"

"She's in New York for two weeks, we have the whole place to ourselves." I stepped inside the unit, Jonah, the only real friend I had here on the Rock meant a lot to me. At first, I didn't want to tell Jonah my problems, but as I sat down I knew that I had to tell someone. "Look, Jonah, after I bought my car, I've had the strangest things happen to me."

"Go on Walters, I'm listening."

"You see, Jonah, I'm mixed up with a drug dealer and the Black Market. The reason I haven't been in touch with you is that I've been married for 2 months, and I've been running all over the place." Jonah soaked it all in before commenting: "Walters, I've always known you to be a bit naïve, but tell me how did you get involved with a drug dealer?"

"They forced me Jonah, and they threatened my wife's life!"

"Who threatened your wife's life Walters, this doesn't sound right."

"Yakuza, Jonah." Jonah sobered a bit. Even the slick New Yorker knew that Yakuza meant business over here on the Island. "Walters, is there any way I can help you?" I looked at my friend with pleading eyes. "Yes, Jonah loan me $20,000 so I can help my wife while I go on the exercise." Jonah didn't flinch, but smiled and stood up. "You know Walters, ordinarily I'd tell you to screw yourself, but I believe you. Excuse me, I'll be right back."

Jonah came back moments later with a personal check. "Walters, I'm giving you this in good faith, but I want you to promise me, that you'll use it wisely."

"I promise Jonah."

"Semper Fi Marine!" Jonah, although not knowing the urgency that I needed to get to Yuriko took my keys before saying: "Come on let's get you back to your wife, where do you live?"

"I live with my wife's mother."

"How on earth did you manage that Walters?"

"Charm my friend, charm." Jonah laughed and patted me on the back. "You know Walters, you have grown a lot these past few months, and you appear more shrewd."

"I hope that's a good thing Jonah."

"So far Walters, just don't cross anyone, you're in a hell of a fix." I could see that Jonah was worried for me and to be seen with me, but the tough Marine would not let fear dominate him. We jumped in Jonah's Chevy and headed out. Jonah carefully looked in the rear-view mirror as he drove. "Walters, did Yakuza threaten you in any way?"

"No, they just let me know that they knew my wife and that I was being watched."

"Do you sell drugs Walters?"

"No Jonah, I'm an errand boy, I deliver them."

"I see." Jonah relaxed a bit and continued to drive. I gave him directions to Mary's home. We sat in his car for a minute. "So this is the setup, huh Walters? Nice."

"Thanks Jonah, I leave Friday, give me your address and I'll keep you abreast of everything."

"Yeah, be sure and do that Walters, I want to make sure you get back in one piece." We shook hands and I got out of the car. "Thanks a million Jonah, you're a life saver."

"Walters, I consider you to be one of my better friends, remember that!"

I stepped out of the way and saluted as Jonah drove off. I felt a little relieved that I had told Jonah of my dilemma, now I could breathe easier. As I headed for the door, I tried to understand Omi's logic. She acted as though she was ashamed or something. Then it hit me; maybe she had been ashamed the way it ended. I knocked and Yuriko quickly answered. She had been waiting for me: "Where's your car Walters?"

"I'm letting my friend take care of it while I'm on the exercise." Yuriko took me by the hand, "I'm sorry the way I behaved earlier Walters, but I don't want to go to Mainland, I'll wait for you right here in Okinawa."

"Yuriko, I want you to be safe and the only way is for you to be with me."

"I know Walters, but I feel safe here with Momma son." I knew it to be fruitless to argue with Yuriko; maybe it was best that she stayed here with Mary. "Yuriko, I'm going to put some money into our checking account at the Credit Union, I want you to have money if you need it, but don't use it unless you have too."

"Okay Walters. Are you hungry?"

"I'm starved, what's for dinner Yuriko, let's get to it."

"I made some mushroom soup." I tried to stay positive, but mushroom soup, damn! Beside myself, I still went to eat it; I didn't want to upset my love. "Walters, you eat and get to bed you're leaving early in the morning okay?"

"Yes dear, I'll eat and get some rest." I tasted the mushroom soup, hmm; good, and it had some meat in it. I dug in surprised by the taste of the meal.

I quickly ate and went into the bedroom and prepared for bed. Yuriko straightened the kitchen before joining me in the bedroom. As she entered, she gave me a quizzical look: "Walters, I know you're seeing other girls, but that's not what makes me mad."

"What makes you mad Yuriko?" I asked perplexed at her knowledge of my dealings.

"I'm mad because you're leaving so soon, I know you're not coming back." Yuriko then started softly sobbing. "Look Yuriko, I'd come back for you even if they shipped me to America. I love you, Yuriko." I got out of bed and went to hold my lady. She shook with tension. "Listen Yuriko, I'll write you and call you too, don't think like that, I'll be back I promise." Yuriko looked deep into my eyes. She relaxed and went limp in my arms. "I believe you Walters, my momma son doesn't believe you're coming back." Yuriko took off her light blue nightgown. "Where's everyone Yuriko?"

"Visiting relatives Walters." Yuriko gave me a mischievous look. I caught on real quick. "Don't look at me like that young lady, I know what's on your mind."

"Come here Walters." Yuriko fell on the bed; I went in after her. After all I had been through today, I still had plenty left for my young vixen.

We loved for seemingly hours. Out of sheer exhaustion I had to stop our love sessions: "Yuriko, please, I can't take it anymore, I'm spent." Yuriko still insisted on kissing me; I let her have her way. I couldn't believe the sexual animal that I had become. It appeared that Okinawa turned out to be a den of passion. Although I relished my pleasure here, Filson turned out to be the dark horse I couldn't forget. If anything, I bet he'd send his drugs to me over in Mainland if he could. As I held my lover I worried for her safety, for that matter my safety concerned me also.

I got up at 0200 hours and prepared everything to travel to Kadena Air Base. I'd call a Cab to get me to the Base. I showered, put on my camouflage utilities and prepared my items. Yuriko awakened and watched me get my gear ready. She got out of bed to hold me. "Please come back Walters, I like you very much."

"I will darling; nothing will stop me from your love." We hugged for several minutes and I had to release my girl. At this hour it would be hard to get a Cab, but I had plenty of time. "Yuriko, I'm walking down the Street to get a Cab, I'll be back."

"Okay, Walters, I will wait here." I kissed Yuriko and headed out. I felt as light as a feather from all the passion. I probably held no fluids in my reproductive organs, yet if felt like sugar cane in my stomach. I walked no more than fifty yards when I spotted a Cab. I jumped in and then went to get my things.

After packing my gear in the Cab, I went inside to say one last goodbye. Mary and Kim were still gone. Yuriko appeared to handle it better now that she trusted me coming back. "I'll see you as soon as I can Yuriko, I love you."

"I will wait here Walters, I will miss you." We hugged again then I tearfully retreated out of the door and got in the Cab. I had shut the door on the way out and Yuriko didn't open it. "To Kadena Honcho."

"G.I. go home?"

"No, G.I. go to Mainland Japan."

"Nice place, lotta girls for American men."

"I can't wait to see them Honcho." The Cab driver flipped down his register and we were off to Kadena. I had just realized that despite my indiscretions I loved Yuriko deeply, but I couldn't take my mind off Omi. The way she just ran in the Club like that. Then it hit me like an explosion. Omi was the woman in the large picture I observed at the Bar in Naha! I wondered just who it was that I had the pleasurable liaison with and would I see her again. I tried to make a mental note of the Bar for future reference.

CHAPTER THIRTEEN
MR. STEWART

    I took my gear out of the cab, paid the honcho who wished me well and I lugged everything into Kadena's small but vital Airport. There was still traffic at this hour. I checked in the manifest and they took my luggage. Keeping my overnight bag I went and had a seat; I tried to watch whatever it showed on the television in the waiting room. F.E.N. played some old war movies, which didn't interest me so I assumed the sitting position and put my cover over my eyes and tuned everything out. Even though I tried I couldn't shake the memory of everything that I had been through on Okinawa out of my mind. I had grown into a sexually mature person. Back in Nebraska, I liked women, but I never imagined the pleasures hidden deep within them. Sure, I've kissed high school girls on numerous occasions, but I never took it to the hilt. Here on the Rock, I slept with two women on the same night! As for Yuriko, I wanted to stay with her, but I knew giving up immorality would prove difficult if not impossible, but If Yuriko insisted I'd try.

Filson on the other hand had completely surprised me. He had picked me out to use for his drug selling. I couldn't understand why Filson did what he did. To move his drugs was obvious, but he must have had some kind of method before I came along and to trap me into being a runner, I shuddered trying to shut out getting caught. I hadn't been in touch with my father, I felt too ashamed to do it. He'd probably disown me if he knew that I was a part of these illegal activities. Black Market was one thing, but drugs! I wanted to cry out yet age taught me one thing; life went on it never stopped, not even for me. My thoughts drifted to Omi and our brief encounter. I never fathomed things to turn out like they did. By chance looking for a place to kill time and there it happened. A businesswoman to boot; what really shocked me is when I found an address in Mainland in my wallet. I knew it had to be Omi. I did everything possible to keep Yuriko from finding the two addresses from Cameko and Omi. I felt that maybe I'd try to locate them and maybe I wouldn't, time would tell. I tried to rest my mind, but it kept pushing the past months in front of me. Jonah, my friend, had really impressed me. He didn't ask for anything in return and he didn't expect me to give him a long drawn out story about my problems. One thing about Mr. Jonah Crockett was that he appeared to be at perfection with his personality. Monique had really been good for him. And him becoming a dad, I felt very proud for my friend. I wished him well; I chuckled thinking of Sally and how I tried to get back at Filson. Maybe he knew and didn't care, one thing is for sure is he had access to many women, which sort of surprised me. Even though all of Filson's women were ladies of ill repute, they still looked good. I felt an erection coming on thinking of Sally, so young and naïve. She didn't realize what she had gotten herself into and to be trapped in that lifestyle, she had grown up fast. While my mind kept pushing memories to my conscience, I thought of my dad again. Now I understood why dad wanted me to leave the Rock. A small Island, but there's so much to get into, dad knew me to be a man who had little experience about the ways of the world, and he didn't want me to be exposed to this kind of life, but I wanted to know life this way and no one had the right to stop me; dad or no dad.

I must have sat there for an hour or so before someone tapped me on the leg, it was Dunbar. "Hey, Walters, wake up, we're leaving early!"

"Are you serious?" The look on Dunbar's face reiterated his statement. I quickly gathered myself and grabbed my overnight bag and went to stand in line. Sure enough it was announced that a flight was leaving for Mainland at 0500 hours. I stood behind Dunbar in the relatively short line. "How long have you been here Dunbar?"

"About an hour, I kept my eye on you Walters, I figured you'd be tired with your wife and all."

"Thanks Dunbar, yeah, this life of mine I stay busy if you know what I mean." Dunbar laughed and replied: "You know, I'm impressed Walters, I thought by now you'd peter out you know, give in to the pressure."

"What are you saying Dunbar?"

"You know Walters, drink excessively or pick up other bad habits, but you have appeared to hold your own. Of course you probably spend a lot of money, but that's expected." I dare not tell Dunbar that my pushing drugs covered a lot of my expenses, let him come to his own conclusion about the matter, the least knowledge I shared the better. The line begin to move and we quickly boarded the Flying Tiger 747. It appeared this was a stopover for the huge beast and we'd fly to several other Islands before going to Mainland.

Dunbar and I boarded and decided to sit together. I put away my bag and tried to get comfortable. "Walters, did you ever hear from Madison again?"

"No I haven't Dunbar, why?"

"I heard the latest from Natalie and she told me Madison was discharged from the Marines and that she went back to Nebraska."

"Did Natalie mention anything else?"

"Yes, she says that Madison thinks you're the father, but she won't push it. Madison feels she let you down by sleeping with Thorn."

"You know Dunbar, I never really felt that Madison was the girl for me. I had met Yuriko before I started dating Madison." Dunbar sat quiet for a moment than answered: "Walters, you have some touch with the ladies, I sometimes wanted to hang out with you, but I'm very serious about saving money and purchasing my own home."

"I remember you telling me this before Dunbar. Now I understand your frugal approach. It's all or nothing Dunbar, do or die, kill or be killed." We both laughed at the humorous but true slogan of the Marines. Dunbar, a Marine with a purpose, never lost sight of his goal. He must have really wanted a home badly because he denied himself practically everything so far here on Okinawa. I bet he even refused to purchase a Motel for he and Natalie to have a good time. Yeah, Dunbar was driven for success, and looking at him I understood why. A short, but bullish man, Dunbar had to have all angles covered to keep a woman's attention. Anyway, I respected the integrity of the man. We both settled in our seats and prepared to leave Okinawa, at least for the time being.

We made a stop over in Korea and picked up it appeared hundreds of military personnel. Now the Tiger held its maximum capacity. We went into the sky once again. I really enjoyed the craft taking off on the runway. It happens so quickly with your head being pulled into the seat during the crafts accent. We flew for several hours and then we landed. This time it landed at Yokota Air Force Base. I grabbed my overnight bag to disembark along with Dunbar and we headed off the jet. When I made it into the lobby two Military Police stopped Dunbar and I. The taller one said: "Are you Walters and Dunbar?"

"Yes, we are." I answered a bit startled at the commotion. The two Police ushered us to get our luggage then whisked us out of the terminal. I looked over at Dunbar, who appeared to be frightened out of his wits. They drove us over to a part of the Base that held the temporary quarters. The Sergeant spoke first: "You are to stay here until further notice Marines!" He gave us a key and the two Air Force Personnel left quickly. "What was that all about Walters?"

"I have no idea Dunbar, your guess is as good as mine." Scared, but flexible, I put my gear down and sat on one of the four beds in the room. "Well Dunbar, we might as well make the best of this."

"Sure Walters." Dunbar begin to watch me kind of suspicious and I knew why. I didn't want to accept it, but I had the feeling that all of this was behind Filson and my transporting drugs for him. I lay down and surprisingly slept. I woke up to someone knocking on the door. I got up to open it; it was an Air Force Police. "Marine, get your buddy and prepare for chow, we'll be waiting outside."

"Yes Sergeant." I looked at my watch, 0730 hours. We had slept through the night. I woke up slumbering Dunbar, who awakened with spittle coming out of his mouth. "Dunbar, let's get ready for chow." Dunbar did his best to collect himself. "Damn, Walters, you mean we slept all night!"

"I'm surprised too Dunbar, now let's get some chow, I'm starved." Dunbar went into the head first to prepare himself. I didn't bother changing my utilities I'd do that after eating. We both washed our faces and tried to rearrange our uniforms as best as possible. The military police took us to a rather large and orderly chow hall and stayed with us as we got our breakfast. We ate in silence rather quickly and then followed our escorts back to the temporary quarters. "Marines, you are ordered to stay here in the room until further notice!" The military police shut the door behind him. Dunbar went and flopped on his bunk. "You know Walters, these are some nice quarters. The Air Force really knows how to live it up." I had to admit that these quarters exceeded my expectations. Even though they had been built to sleep four, it didn't hurt the fact that plenty of space still remained to move around the room. "Hey Dunbar, how'd you like that good ole Air Force chow?"

"Great, I mean they have civilian cooks and everything; I could really get into eating here regularly."

"I bet you could. I'm still clueless as to what's going on Dunbar."

"Come on Walters, you know it's behind whatever you did on the Rock, but what I don't understand is why I'm here."

"Good point. I can't answer that either." I felt for Dunbar, if that indeed was the case. Why he had to be pulled into all of this, or he knew something he never mentioned. I decided to question him. "Dunbar is there something you're not telling me?" Dunbar didn't respond.

"Dunbar I'm waiting." Finally, Dunbar answered:

"Walters, I know one thing, that they were on to you for sometime on the Rock."

"On to me for what Dunbar?"

"Word gets around Walters. People knew you pushed for Filson, but no one would challenge him. They figured you spent so much money on whores that you needed the extra money." Dunbar then chuckled at his comment. It stung like a razor, but it rang true. "Who all knew Dunbar?"

"Those Marines in the know, Walters, to put you at ease everyone didn't know and if they did they never talked. From what Natalie say's Madison was sent back to the States because of it."

"Are you serious?"

"Just rumors Walters. Anyway, that may not be the reason we're here, it could be something else you know."

"No Dunbar it all adds up. We both supposedly coming on an exercise to Mainland only to be locked up in this room my involvement with Filson has to be it." Dunbar appeared to be a pawn in this. He had nothing to do with anything, but He was in it up to the neck. I lay on my rack trying to lay a finger on everything. Why on earth would I have to leave the Rock and be put in this situation?

As I thought I became a little frightened: Were they going to lock me up?" Did someone snitch? Did Dunbar know more than he let on?" The questions tore at me. As time for chow rolled around both Dunbar and I had changed clothes and showered and got into clean uniforms. This time we got a lunch bag to eat in the rooms. We both ate in silence. Pressure began to mount. Dunbar became very silent, although he watched me closely. After lunch I took a short nap. A banging on the door awakened me. This time when I opened it a Marine lance Corporal stood there: "lance Corporal Walters?"

"Yes."

"I'm lance Corporal Paul Stewart, I'm from military Intelligence."

"What are we supposed to do lance Corporal?"

"Let me in for one thing." I motioned for the squared away looking Marine to enter. He did and sat down on one of the chairs in the room. "Walters, at ease. I'm just here to relay some information to you."

"What kind of information Stewart?"

"Walters, we are currently ready to pull the rug from underneath a Marine whose name happens to be Maurice Filson." I tightened up a bit. Stewart noticed and put his hands up. "Hold on Walters, we know all about you so there is no need to be afraid. You see we know that you were pressured into working for Mr. Filson."

"How do you know that, Stewart?" He shrugged and smiled then looked directly at me:

"Walters, you've been watched very closely since you've purchased your car and what really helps your cause is that we had a plant."

"A plant!" I asked suspiciously.

"Yes, one of the men who worked for Filson was a plant."

"Which one?" I asked to see if I could identify him.

"The one that watched Filson punch you in the stomach over Cameko's." Dunbar sat there intently soaking everything up like a dry sponge. "How long was he a plant Stewart?"

"For almost a year Walters. Whether you realize it or not Walters, you were involved in some heavy shit and if Naval Intelligence wasn't so lenient toward you, you'd be going down with Mr. Filson." I didn't respond to the soft-spoken Marine. He wore enlisted men stripes, but he appeared to be an above average intelligent man. Perhaps he wore the in sigma to have a cover. I decided to risk asking a question that now weighed heavily on my mind. "Stewart, why didn't they bust me?" Stewart looked longingly at me. He appeared to be tired. A young man with old man responsibilities; "Walters, in the world you played in you wouldn't stand a chance in. You know what saved you?"

"What's that Stewart?"

"The fact that you went along with Filson. Did you know that three Marines have come up missing that had dealings with Mr. Filson and they haven't been found to this day."

"Stewart, just who the hell is Filson?"

"Walters, Filson is a convict who somehow slipped through the cracks. He has some very powerful connections and they make at least six figures here on the Rock."

"Where does the Navy plan on doing to Filson, Stewart?"

"For one thing Walters, Filson's connections are all over the Orient, as a matter of fact we have a National Guard General involved." Stewart saw an open bunk and went for it. "I might as well make use of this rack gentlemen." Stewart lay down and continued oratating. "Yes, men, as we speak, Naval Intelligence has Filson in custody and they're grilling him. You know Walters, he's a sharp man, but he'd never figure you were pulled away to catch him. I believe he thinks you're clean."

"What are they going to do with Filson, Stewart?"

"They are going to turn him over to Japanese authorities. They are talking execution or twenty years hard labor." I winced; that could have easily been me. I understood Filson to be an unusual person, but he turned out to be a menace. I tried to understand things. A ring of military men involved in a drug cartel. Filson liked what he did and now he had to play the piper. I had another question I needed to ask Stewart. "What's Dunbar doing here Stewart?"

"He's here so Filson couldn't piece things together. He'd have known you were being taken away because of him. Now all he can claim is that you have been sent on an exercise and we want it to stay that way. You know he still has ties to the Yakuza."

"That's another thing Stewart, my wife!"

"Don't worry Walters, she is being watched too. Japanese authorities are trying to arrest perpetrators who have anything to do with the drug deals even though they are The U.S. citizens. The Yakuza have completely backed off, they don't want any confrontation with Japanese authorities." Stewart let his statement sink in and I accepted it. I had no idea how deep I was in this ring. A drug cartel! That really blew my mind. Cameko had saw the danger and escaped. I hope she was all right. The three of us lie on our bunks and contemplating things. Several minutes went by then Stewart stood up and walked over to me. "There is some information I need from you Walters?"

"I need proof that you actually transported narcotics for Filson." I didn't hesitate to answer: "I'm positive I had drugs because I looked into the contents several times. Marijuana and cocaine."

"Are you sure Walters?"

"Positive Stewart; now tell me about the General involved in this." Stewart sighed and went and sat back on the rack: "Walters, General Ivan Brausenhower has been living in the Philippines for some seven years. He is a very wealthy man whose family is loaded. His father is from Germany and he reportedly is a Stock Broker. Ivan shot through the ranks and became a Brigadier General.

He left the United States after twenty years in the Guard for Manila and he became underworld. He has hundreds of men working for him in the drug trade. As you know the Philippines Islands is loaded with high potency marijuana. Word is that Ivan gets cocaine directly from Columbia." I took in a deep breath at the fact presented before me, but I still needed to know how Filson got into all of this. "Stewart where did Filson come into the picture?" Stewart steadied himself before stating: "Walters, Filson is tied to the mob in America. Apparently, he has been committing illegal acts long before he joined the Marines. He had his records sealed, that's how he was able to enlist in the Corps without being discovered. Dunbar, listening the whole time suddenly burst out laughing. He laughed uncontrollably for a few moments then straightened himself. Stewart, perplexed at the outburst waited for a reply: "What's so funny Marine!"

"Sorry fellas, I was thinking of an incident Natalie and I had with Filson." Curious I had to know: "What kind of incident Dunbar?"

"Well, once at the Club, Filson approached Natalie and asked her to dance. She refused and Filson didn't take it too well. He began yelling at Natalie calling her a stuck-up bitch. Anyway, four white Marines escorted him out of the Club and Filson was some kind of angry." Not really perceiving the point, nonetheless, I didn't question Dunbar. Stewart wasn't finished with us. "Look Marines when this drug raid is complete we want to bring Ivan Brausenhowser to justice. He lives in the Mountains and he's hard to catch. He has a lot of networks here in the Orient."

There was nothing to do but gasp at everything. Filson, the tough criminal that he portrayed now was going to rot away in a Japanese prison. Not the type to smirk at another's pain, still, I felt for him. I made roughly $5000 delivering drugs and most of it had been spent on frivolous living. Plus with me buying the items for Mary I had went through some heavy cash. Stewart, still not finished sat on his rack writing information. He wrote for 10 minutes and then he closed his ledger. "Look boys, I'd love to stay and chat but I have a plane to catch."

"Where are you going Stewart?"

"We have to arraign Mr. Filson in order to have enough information to turn him over to Japanese officials. With your statement Walters I think we have him."

"Will he know I snitched Stewart?"

"No, he'll be charged, you won't need to take the witness stand." Relieved, I shook Stewart's hand. "What now Stewart?"

"You both will be here for a while then they may transfer you to a Marine Base for a couple of months, in any case you won't be going to Okinawa for a while." Stewart then wished us well and departed. Dunbar who was privileged to witness this spectacle looked at me and smiled saying: "Walters, I'm not one to meddle, but why on earth did you keep selling for Filson you could have said no!"

"Dunbar, they threatened my wife and I was warned about snitching too."

"You know Walters that lance Corporal Stewart is one scary mutha."

"Yeah, I bet he kicks ass and takes names."

"I agree Walters, he's not the biggest person, but he appears very wiry and quick."

"I bet he has his hands full with the ladies."

"No, Walters, that's your expertise. You were known on Camp Kinser as the guy who deflowered Madison and started her immoral ways."

"Dunbar, Madison is a Marine, she has her own life to live, besides, she offered it to me."

"I know Walters, but there were more than a few women interested in you, but you didn't know it did you?"

"No, I can't say I did Dunbar, that's news to me." Dunbar appeared to come down off of his cloud. "I'm resting until chow Walters, this has been some information that will affect me the rest of my life."

"I agree." I said and tried to get comfortable and make sense of it all.

After chow we received another visit. This one from a battle-ready Gunnery Sergeant. He came in the room and sat down before saying anything. He looked around the room apparently for cleanness. Then Gunny gave the commanding order: "Get you gear ready Marines tomorrow we're headed to Main side, Mount Fuji." Both Dunbar and I yelled in unison: "Yes sir!" The gunny pleased at our neatness left the room without saying anything else.

We realized it was past chow time and we hadn't eaten yet, but there was no way I'd question anyone now. It was fact I had been sent here because of my involvement with Filson. I counted my lucky stars that I had not been busted and locked away. Yes, I did transport drugs, but I never meant to do it maliciously. Filson recruited me and out of fear I did it. I realized my dad just might find out about my past and if he did, he'd be very disappointed in me. At this point I loved my father, but I realized he and I were on different pages in life. Wikenberg had told me that my dad would be a politician, yet I hadn't heard anything else about it. No word from my dad shocked me somewhat. Although we had grown apart when I didn't want to travel with him as a young child. I wanted to stay with grandma. Dad, a tough Army Officer never had time to explain the things of life incidental to being a man. He never explained the power of sex and ladies that were below a certain level in society. Maybe he figured I'd catch on and automatically know these things. In any case I had to learn on my own. I counted my blessings for having Yuriko. I felt we had a good life together since we're both so young there appeared to be more than enough time for kids. As I contemplated my life there was a knock on the door. Relieved, I knew it had to be our evening chow.

CHAPTER FOURTEEN
FUJI

We had been aboard the Base for 2 months. Any day now we were scheduled to go back to Okinawa. Dunbar and I had been assigned to Mess duty and Maintenance detail. It wasn't glamorous, but here on Mainland there are plenty of things to get into. Dunbar as usual, stayed aboard the Base, which didn't bother me much, but his complaining of being homesick really got to me. Word was that Dunbar would be sent to the States soon, we both knew why it turned out that Dunbar knew several associates of Filson who told him things. Naval Security had become worried that Dunbar could really damage my cover and get me injured or worse. I never confronted Dunbar, but he openly discussed it in our two-man room here on Base, which I duly noted. Lance Corporal Stewart had stopped by periodically to check on us. He kept us abreast of Filson's current status. So far, they had captured 15 people on Okinawa alone; still no Brausenhower. Stewart said that Brausenhower had been informed by his contacts and fled the Island. A tricky man indeed, Filson as of now still was being held by U.S. Authorities. It turned out that when Filson knew he would be turned over to Japanese authorities, he sang like a canary.

That surprised me I thought Filson to be a tough hard-nosed man, who could handle himself in any situation, not this cry baby who feared institutions. Stewart also said it's likely that Filson might be transferred to America and released. He had snitched on two Air Force Officers who had been flying the drugs to the Rock, this set well with Naval Security because apparently they promised Filson immunity if he gave names of important people. It also turned out that Filson was not involved in murder after all. I felt cheated somewhat; here I had been transferred away from Yuriko and now this. Stewart said everything now rested on Marine Corps Brass on what to do with me. The Brass still angry at my actions didn't feel too keen on letting me walk, but Navy Brass out ranked them so I escaped prosecution. Still, leaving the Rock so abruptly and to top it off they released Filson! I cringed when Stewart informed me about these things.

I had written both Omi and Cameko. Omi had written back and had sent me a letter telling me to meet her at the train station at Gotemba in two weeks. I called Yuriko and wrote and she couldn't wait until I got back to her. For sport I went to a local Bar down the street from the Base. I had met a married woman named Gatsuki who I drank with on several occasions. An older woman, Gatsuki had to be at least fifty. Still attractive and shapely, Gatsuki carried a few wrinkles, but nothing serious. She still had all of her teeth, which was more than I could say about most women who frequented these spots. Gatsuki would always tell me about the great Mount Fuji. It still had snow at the top of the huge crater. The Volcano had been dormant for years and it mainly turned out to be a tourist attraction. This part of Japan still held its own beauty, some parts were even breath taking. Gatsuki drank a bit too much, but she turned out to be a real companion. We would meet on Friday's after work and talk until the Bar closed. Today, however, Gatsuki planned on meeting me at the Bar after work and she promised to ask the Momma son to let us borrow one of the bedrooms upstairs. I got up Friday morning hoping the day went by quick.

Today turned out to be pleasant to say the least. After payday we got the afternoon off and we didn't have to return back to our detail until

Monday. Dunbar wanted to stay aboard Base and get an extra session of physical training. I went to the Exchange and got a fifth of Segrams Seven; I wanted to be ready for Gatsuki at any cost. To be extra prepared I exchanged for $200 worth of yen. I didn't use much of the stuff in Okinawa, but here on the Mainland, yen held its own. After eating chow, I wrote Letters to Jonah and Omi. I wanted to touch Base with Jonah and let him know I was okay. I had to keep Omi informed so that we could get together in two weeks.

After writing the letters I decided to shower and get into civilian clothing. Hanging around this Base didn't matter at first, but after a period of time it got down right depressing. Today the Sun did brighten the day so that wasn't the problem. The thing that bugged me most is that there were not many things to do except work out and when I didn't do that, things really sucked. Tonight would help a bit it depended on what Gatsuki wanted to do. Her being married didn't stop her from seeing or flirting heavily with me. Her English wasn't great but I understood most of what she said. I had not had a woman in sometime. At first, I wanted to stay loyal to Yuriko, but that proved to be far out of my control. Fidelity is one thing, yet buildup is another and at my age I had quite a few seeds swimming around in my tank, it should be nice to empty it in Gatsuki.

1700 hours rolled around and I headed out to the Bar. Most Marines at this hour had Tokyo on their minds. I had the decency to at least tell Yuriko that I never stepped foot on Tokyo so far. That might defuse any resistance she offered when I got back to the Rock. I took everything I needed and walked out of the Gate. The Japanese gate Guards waved me through and I cautiously walked by them. Yes, this area by the foot of the Mountain had to be decades behind in time. I would say the late 50's. As I walked Marines were scurrying out of the Gate to catch the Bus that took them to the train station. From there they rode to Tokyo or wherever else they planned on traveling this weekend. I passed the few Bars on the way to meet Gatsuki. The Seagram's made the special noise the liquor makes sloshing around in the bottle. The walk was all down hill as we were still at the foot of the Mountain. Mount Fuji, a spectacle indeed.

When I arrived at the old-fashioned bar, Gatsuki sat on the bench waiting for me:

"Hajimemashite?" (How do you do)

"Konban wa;" (Hello) Gatsuki had taught me some simple greetings in Japanese. Fortunately, she started speaking English. "Walters, you look tired."

"I'm fine Gatsuki, I have been sleeping." I tried to speak so that Gatsuki understood me.

"You sleep, no work today?"

"Yes, I worked and slept."

"Yoku nemure mashita ka?" (You sleep well)

"Wakarimasen;" (I don't understand) Gatsuki smiled and said:

"I try to speak English to you." The Bar was empty at this time. Gatsuki called the momma son over. They conversated for a while and then Gatsuki turned to me. "Momma son say we can use the room all night for $50." Hesitant at first yet I knew I'd do it I agreed. Gatsuki urged me to go upstairs with her, which suited me just fine. We went upstairs and on the way up Gatsuki began pinching me on the bottom. I of course started getting erect. When we got into the small room, I could see that the Bar actually served as a Brothel on the side. Some Americans frequented this Bar, and from the looks of the clientele that worked here, they had few takers. The women were a tad bit over the hill. There were a couple of younger girls and they most assuredly stayed busy during peak hours. Gatsuki begin undressing and I observed anticipating sagging breast, but she surprised me. Her breast, very small and upturned and she had a very flat stomach and fairly decent curves. Her bush, very girlish looking and not a lot of hair, which made me stare lustfully. Gatsuki noticed me and became shy. She covered herself with her hand. I started undressing while Gatsuki took her turn watching. When I was naked, she exclaimed at my member: "Oki-sugi-mass!" (That's to big)

"Oh, no, Gatsuki, I will take my time." When we both stood there naked, I went and embraced Gatsuki. I gently lie her on the floor mat. She didn't appear afraid, just cautious. When I got Gatsuki on her back I parted her legs for her. I worked trying to penetrate her. She lie still during the whole process. Finally, I penetrated her. "Itami-mass;" (It hurts) I assumed that meant hurt, so I slowly pumped trying to let her juices begin to flow. It took a few minutes, but Gatsuki received me. I took it easy on her and the friction led me to an explosive climax. I convulsed while I erupted, the semen gushing forth in volumes. Gatsuki was as tight as Yuriko. I stayed inside of her until I became erect again then I went at the excited and climaxing Gatsuki. The senses became so intense that I had to stop and withdraw. I could tell Gatsuki really enjoyed it because she smiled and stayed close to me. "Walters, you good to me no?"

"Yes Gatsuki, I am." We chuckled and enjoyed the aftermath of sex. When the power hit me, I stood up and took out the Seagram's. Gatsuki called for the momma son, who quickly came up the stairs. Gatsuki gave momma son the $50 and they spoke in Japanese. Momma son left and quickly came back with two cups and some Seven Up. Now I could hear people down stairs laughing and the smell of cigarettes and alcohol. I knew this to be business hours. Gatsuki, after taking the items from Momma son opened the Seagram's and poured us a drink. "We stay long time Walters." Gatsuki said as she sipped her drink. I had prided myself on avoiding too much liquor, but after having sex with Gatsuki, I decided to treat myself. I sipped on the smooth and inviting Seagram's. It felt warm going down. It had been a while since I drank and I wanted to enjoy it.

We drank for over an hour; we still were naked and we enjoyed the privacy. People were coming and going down the stairs, it appeared there was good money being made tonight. I felt the liquor taking a hold of me so I went and lie down. Gatsuki followed suit. She too appeared stoned. As we both lie on the floor close to each other I began caressing Gatsuki's body. She instantly responded by arching her back. I continued caressing her moving down to her spot. She gasped as I began fondling her genitals. Gatsuki, even at 50 still had sex appeal. Surprisingly I begin kissing her. She writhered in pleasure; I had exceeded my limit sexually, so there was no way I could make love, so I brought Gatsuki to climax with my fingers. She went limp quickly afterwards falling asleep in the process. I lay back listening to the crowd and soon I fell asleep.

I came too to the bright and shining Sun. Gatsuki still slept. I nudged her until she opened her eyes. She gathered herself and sat upright on the floor mat. "How long have I been sleeping Walters?"

"All night everyone's gone Gatsuki."

"No, momma son, she stay here with us." I fell back down on the mat:

"I'm hungry Gatsuki."

"I take you home with me and we eat some Japanese food." Alarmed I stopped Gatsuki:

"What about your husband Gatsuki?"

"He with his Japanese girlfriend, he no care!"

"Gatsuki, your friends will see me and tell him." That rang a bell because Gatsuki didn't say anything. Then she thought of something: "You stay here and take shower, I bring some food back okay Walters."

"Okay Gatsuki, I will wait here." Gatsuki got up and dressed and went down the short hallway. Then she came back with a towel and a small bar of soap. "I show you shower Walters." I jumped up and followed Gatsuki down stairs; she led me to a small cubicle. Sure enough there was a small shower. "Thank you Gatsuki. I showered lathering up real well and after rinsing off I stepped out of the shower and dried myself off. Still feeling the effects of the liquor, I took it easy going up the stairs. I dressed and lie down, what the hell, it was Saturday and I had nothing to do all day, so I'd take it easy and see what Gatsuki would bring me back to eat.

She came back a couple of hours later with a Styrofoam container. "Walters I get you something from restaurant."

"Thanks, Gatsuki, I'm very hungry." I took the container and opened it. Rice and bits of chicken, very tasty looking; before I could ask Gatsuki went into her purse and took out a plastic fork. "Take this Walters, it is easy for you." I took the fork and begin eating. Gatsuki appeared to enjoy watching me eat with a fork. I ate until the container was empty. "You very hungry no?"

"Yes, Gatsuki, I'm okay now, thank you." Gatsuki smiled and took the container from me. Felling a bit antsy, but I decided to stick it out and see what Gatsuki and I could get into. Gatsuki came back and stripped to her bra and panties. I did the same and lay down next to her. I caressed her, my hands getting supercharged with Gatsuki's smooth skin. I felt good. She became putty in my hands. A cute woman Gatsuki appeared to be famished for attention. Her husband apparently went for other women and had neglected his wife. I didn't like messing around with married women, but here on the soil of Japan I found that things just didn't go like in America. Japanese loved the idol Buddha and they lived accordingly. As long as I stayed in the Orient, I'd frolic in the mass of flesh available here.

Gatsuki loved me stroking her. She turned this way and that and I concentrated on her bottom. We avoided kissing which would have been a signal that we were serious. I stroked Gatsuki until my arm grew tired, she turned around facing me: "Walters, you like coming here?"

"Yes, Gatsuki I do."

"You want to come next weekend?"

"I won't have money Gatsuki and I have to go home soon."

"When you leave Japan Walters?"

"Very soon Gatsuki, I will stop by and see you and let you know when I leave."

"I might have another friend next week, I work here now."

"What about your husband Gatsuki?"

"He want me to bring in money so I will work. I meet nice guy like you I will like working here."

"I will still come and see you Gatsuki."

"Okay Walters." Gatsuki took my arm and put it underneath her bra. I began to play with her nipple. She jumped and her butt pressed against my member. I felt blood rushing to it. Gatsuki smiled and pushed harder against me. I got rough with her nipple Gatsuki gyrated against me. I enjoyed Gatsuki for the rest of the day. I knew that once I went back to Base it would be business as usual. We played around for several hours until I became exhausted with foreplay. Gatsuki seemed to get a kick out of me pressing against her. Finally, she kicked out of her panties. We shared one last session of lovemaking. Afterwards we cleaned ourselves and I said my goodbyes. I gave me friend a big hug and let her keep the liquor. Gatsuki held her hand out, so I gave her $100. She accepted and wished me a good day. I retreated back to Base to reenergize.

That next Friday came around. I prepared to meet Omi at the train station at Gotemba. I had visited Gatsuki earlier in the week and we had a decent conversation and we maintained our friendship. She never asked for sex again, but she still tried to teach me Japanese. I picked up what I could, but it took time to learn the language like I wanted. Gatsuki informed me that Okinawans were what Americans call hicks. They loved the simple life and I agreed. Still I loved Yuriko dearly and I anticipated being with her, but for now I wanted to talk with Omi and learn from her a few things.

It was 1650 when I caught the Bus down to the Gotemba train station. It would be easy to spot Omi, I still had a good mental image of her. I had worn a pair of slacks and a blue long sleeve shirt. I had a change of clothes just in case and a couple of pair of skivvies. Gatsuki turned out to be more friend than anything else and she, like me, knew that if we had sex too often I'd keep coming to her. She never mentioned it, but me being married bothered her. The lovemaking turned out to be very good, I'd remember my mature lover.

When I got to the train station, I stood out in the open with my overnight bag so that Omi could see me when she came. I waited for 10 minutes before I decided to go and have a seat in the train terminal. Very busy, the terminal teemed with people traveling to and from Gotemba. I ended up waiting for over 30 minutes before someone lightly tapped me on the shoulder. Omi! Shocked that she even showed up I stood and turned around: "Hello Omi, nice to see you."

"Hi Walters, it's been a while. Why don't we buy tickets to Tokyo, I want to take you to my place." Pleased, I went to the ticket counter with Omi and we purchased tickets to Tokyo. As we waited to board the Train, Omi looked me over rather seductively before saying: "I really enjoyed our time we spent together in Okinawa, you know Walters, I thought we'd never see each other again." She waited for a reply and I didn't want to blow this golden opportunity.

"Omi I'm glad I found your address in my wallet before my wife found it. Thanks for thinking about me."

"You know Walters, I didn't want to continue our friendship like this, but I felt so good about your personality that I would have been really hurt not to see you again." I appreciated Omi's perfect English. She had studied very well. I melted listening to her sultry voice. "Omi, I felt so bad that you and I had to part with each other that way. I had tried to remember the club, so that I could come back when I go back to Okinawa." Omi smiled and kissed me on the cheek.

"Walters, now you won't have to wait until you get back to Okinawa, I'm right here."

"Yes, I see." I returned the kiss on the cheek and we held hands. I could feel a bond instantly growing between us. I didn't understand why Oriental women were so sensuous. It baffled me why I became so enflamed with passion in each encounter I had. It felt good, but being no fool, something had to give one day and I'd pay the piper. Even with this knowledge I couldn't help myself. We held hands as we boarded the Train. We received some ominous stares as we did so. I looked at Omi for a reaction and saw none. This relaxed me, so I took my seat next to Omi. The Train appeared rather primitive for Mainland, began making its move down the tracks. Omi snuggled closer to me. "It will take a little over an hour Walters, so make yourself comfortable."

"Thanks Omi, I guess I'll sightsee for a bit."

"No, Walters, it's evening and you might strain your eyes. Wait until tomorrow, I'll take you to some interesting places once we get to Tokyo. Do you like to dance Walters?" I hesitated before answering that question. Now I understood that dancing is not one of my strong points, I didn't want to disappoint Omi. "Look Omi, I'm more of a spectator than anything, but I do like to go out though, it relieves tension if you know what I mean." I gently prodded Omi with my arm. "No I don't know what you mean Walters, why don't you tell me." Omi sounded more surprised than anything and I looked over at her to see the amused expression on her face. "Well, Omi I get relaxed from observing females, the way they dress, their shapes, and the way they carry themselves. It stimulates me to watch, so I never really learned to dance not even in America Omi, as a matter of fact I started going out when I joined the military."

"Is that so Walters, I'm surprised; I thought a big strong guy like you went out all the time."

"Omi my past before the military, I stayed home a lot, studied and sometimes went to worship with my grandmother." Omi really appeared surprised. We both went silent all the while listening to the vibration of the Train lumbering down the tracks. Despite Omi's warning I still looked out of the window to see if I could notice anything spectacular or unusual.

Mainly I saw the shadows of buildings and neighborhood. I then tried to close my eyes and concentrate on my surroundings. I'd say the Train was three quarters full with mostly young people who appeared to be headed for the big city lights of Tokyo. The Train stopped several times before finally stopping in Tokyo. I became instantly amazed at the brilliance of the city. Bright lights boomed on every corner. In all the excitement of seeing the activity I forgot about Omi. Omi had been reflective the whole time since I admitted that I didn't dance. She must have really thought I was a swinger or maybe I carried myself as such. We disembarked the Train and Omi still remained silent. "Is everything okay Omi?"

"Sure, I'm just thinking about what we are going to do since you don't dance or anything, I don't know where to take you."

"Listen Omi I don't mind going out and trying to dance."

"Really Walters?"

"Really."

"Okay then we will go to Roppongi District to one of the Clubs that Americans go to."

"That will be fine Omi." Omi took my hand and we hailed a cab. Here in Tokyo cabs came quickly. We got one within seconds. Omi spoke to the cab driver in Japanese. Soon we were near a disco tech. "You will like this club Walters, lots of Americans come here."

"As long as I'm with you Omi, I don't mind where we go." We went into a Club called Jasper. Very nice and cozy, and when we got to the dance floor it was very crowded. I spoke loud so Omi could hear me. "It's very crowded in her Omi!"

"Yes, it is, would you like to dance?" I took Omi by the arm and went out on the dance floor. Soul music filled the air. I tried to get in rhythm and dance to the beat. Omi was no pro either. We both frolicked on the dance floor having the time of our lives. We must have danced for several songs in a row before Omi put her hands up. "I'm exhausted Walters, let's have a seat." We both looked around the tiny Club for a seat before Omi spotted an empty chair. "Over there Walters!" We quickly walked over to an empty table and sat down before anyone could claim it. "Whew, Walters, I need a break, dancing really makes you tired!"

"I agree Omi." I said as I joined her taking a breather. We sat for a couple of songs and then I decided to get us some refreshment. "I'll be right back Omi." There was a line so I got in and waited my turn.

I ordered us Seven Up a favorite here on the Mainland. I still limited my alcohol intake, it was very easy to like the feeling of inebriation here on the Island especially when one dealt with females. After drinking our drinks, we got back on the dance floor. This time we danced for several hours. My feet ached once we retreated off the floor. "You ready to go Walters, I'm exhausted."

"Sure, I'm tired from all the Soul music, you know it really makes you move. Bumbedy bump bump." Omi laughed at my language. "You're funny Walters, come on let's get down stairs and get a taxi." We slowly left the Club and walked outside looking for a ride. Omi flagged a cab down and we jumped in and Omi gave the driver directions. I closed my eyes and tried to relax while the driver took us to our destination. Omi sensing my intentions didn't talk as we rode in the cab. After twenty minutes, we stopped. "Walters, I thought you may have wanted to rest at a hotel before we go to my place."

"Where do you live Omi?"

"Near Yokohama."

"I'm not very familiar with Mainland yet, you'll have to excuse me."

"I understand Walters, but just keep trying you'll learn one day." Omi paid the driver in yen and we stepped out of the cab. The driver waved as he drove off. The hotel very nice awaited us. "Omi I can pay if you like?"

"No, that's fine Walters, I'll pay." We went through the glass doors of the hotel called the Asia Central of Japan. Omi went to the front desk and requested a room. The clerk ignored me and took the yen from Omi and gave her a key. Omi silently took the key and led me through a doorway and up some stairs. This hotel happened to be very nice. I slowly climbed the stairs and followed Omi as she went to our room. "This is a popular hotel for visitors Walters, I hope you like it."

"Anything will suit me tonight Omi, I'm beat." Omi giggled and we finally got to our room. Omi opened the door and I was mildly surprised by the nice neat rooms. A double bed sat in the middle of the room and I made a beeline for it. I tried to talk to Omi, but I could barely keep my eyes open. "Walter, would you like some tea to help you relax?"

"Sure Omi." Omi got on the phone and ordered room service. Within minutes a young girl brought up a silver platter with two crystal cups. She quickly sat the try down and left without speaking. My eyes being nearly shut, I clumsily took a cup of tea from Omi. I quickly drank it hoping to get some much-needed rest. Within seconds I quickly lost conscience.

Hours later I woke up. I couldn't believe it, my hands were bound behind my back and I was blindfolded. As I tried to sit up a hand pushed me back down. "Who is it!" I yelled trying to identify my captors. "It looks like your friend tricked you Mr. Walters."

"What friend?"

"Miss. Omi Susuki." A little upset but curious I wanted to know how Omi could trick me. "How did she trick me?"

"She brought you to us!" Whoever it was had a point, I lay here bound and the last person I saw was Omi. I felt drugged so Omi must have taken me here to trap me. "Why would she do this?" I yelled beginning to panic.

"Have you forgotten so quickly Mr. Walters, you remember our deal, don't you?"

"What deal are you talking about, I never made a deal!"

"In Okinawa, a Mr. Filson, do you remember him." I remained silent now it all came to me. The Yakuza must have got involved in this and targeted me. "Where am I." I said wanting to know whom the smooth velvety voice Oriental man I talked too was. "Don't worry Mr. Walters, you are in a place where no one will find you unless we want them too."

"Look if you don't release me right now, you're in big trouble, I'm a U.S. Marine!" I tried to intimidate my captors. "That won't do you any good Mr. Walters, no one will find you. You can scream and kick and still no one will hear you." I tried to stand but my hands were tied to my legs. "It's useless Mr. Walters, you can't escape." After the voice spoke, I heard a door close shut almost sounding like a patio door or screen door. It felt like I was in a metal room or something, it was very cold to the touch. I had been in some pretty rough spots, but this time I brought the farm. All I could do was wait I didn't know how much time I had, but I had to mentally prepare to escape if the situation presented itself.

CHAPTER FIFTEEN
THE GIFT

I mustered up my Marine Corps discipline so I wouldn't break under the tremendous pressure that gripped my brain. I didn't want to yell out knowing that weakness may be detrimental to my survival. Everything begins to flash before my eyes. Yuriko, Omi, and Cameko; was everything planned so that Yakuza had control over my actions? I dreaded thinking that Yuriko had anything to do with this! She couldn't have, I pushed the thoughts out of my mind. It must have been daylight because now it started getting hot. The metal caught heat from the Sun and reverberated on my exposed skin. I didn't know how long I could take this, yet I understood I had no choice. With the blindfold tight around my eyes and my hands bound, my muscles started aching. What lay ahead of me only my captors knew.

I had been in this condition for so long it seemed like eternity had passed. No one came and opened the door and I couldn't help but wonder if they were coming back or did they leave me here to die. The air started getting stuffy and thick; I begin to feel feint, I desperately needed some fresh air. I wouldn't last much longer like this. At least the heat did not become unbearable; I had to be grateful for that. To make matters worse, hunger gnawed at my stomach and I felt the acid of fear rising up to my throat. My life flashed before my eyes and then while all the horrors of my reality flashed before my eyes I lost consciousness.

Awakened by a loud noise, someone was trying to open the door. Panic stricken yet too weak to do anything, I waited for my end. "Walters!" Someone yelled. It was a familiar voice, but I was so exhausted a feeble, 'yeah' came out.

"Don't worry Marine, we'll get you out of here!" Barely conscience I tried to smile, but my lips were cracked. I could only watch in delight as the blind fold and the ropes were taken off. "Can you walk Walters?" I didn't answer and I tried to focus, but my vision had blurred, my throat parched now prevented me from replying. The Marine picked me up and put me in the fireman's carry and carried me outside. Even though I was extremely weak, the night air felt pleasant to my soaking wet sweaty body. I was carried to a vehicle and put in the back seat. I lost consciousness again and I stayed that way until I awakened in a bed. The room, neat and cozy had to be a hospital and it was American; but where? Intravenous needles were in both arms. I felt better, but I was still a little weak. I focused on a woman; it was a Nurse in a Navy uniform. "Hey Marine, how do you feel?"

"Terrible Maam, but I'll manage."

"Good, now maybe you can eat a little bit."

"Where am I Nurse?"

"You're at Yokoska Naval Station Marine."

"How did I get here Nurse?"

"You were carried in here on a stretcher about three hours ago. You were out so we put you in a bed and gave you some fluids. Now open wide and take this chow."

After eating I felt tons better. I had begun to get my strength back and my vision started getting better. As I lay there thanking my stars, Lance corporal Stewart came into the room. "Hey, Walters, how are you?"

"Much better Stewart, but how the hell did I get here?"

"I brought you here earlier, whoever it was that snatched you had left you out in a gardeners shed in the middle of nowhere to rot Marine."

"Well then, how the hell did you find me Stewart?"

"We had a Japanese agent follow you to Tokyo. You are very lucky Mr. Walters, he did an excellent job."

"Where's Omi?"

"Your girlfriend is not what you think Walters, they paid her or threatened her, whatever reason, and she set you up rather thoroughly." I couldn't believe Omi could do something like this, but I had to admit, my penis had been thinking for me and it practically cost me my life. "Tell me something Stewart, how long did I stay in the room you found me in?"

"You stayed in there for three days Walters. We had to wait until they abandoned you before we were able to make a move, otherwise they'd have murdered you outright." Stewart had a grim look on his face. Murdered, I still had trouble believing my life was in danger. Who'd have thought that the Orient could be so dangerous? I had heard of the dangerous Snakes called Habu, but this situation didn't add up. Why did they want me out of the way? Curious I had to ask Stewart. "Tell me something Stewart, why did they want to get rid of me?"

"For one thing Walters, you unknowingly brought down several key figures in the drug trade, you hit a main vein." I lay there soaking in the message. Filson knew some key drug dealers and they wanted to get revenge. Omi must have been watched as well and got caught up in their web. Either way I know longer felt safe here on the Mainland. "So what's going to happen now Stewart?"

"Well Walters, as soon as you get your strength you're going home. We are taking you off the Rock."

"What about my wife?"

"That's up to you Walters, you can take her with you or not, it's your call."

"She's my wife for crying out loud." I couldn't leave Yuriko behind; we grew to be a part of each other. "When will I leave Stewart?"

"You are going to be taken back to Camp Fuji, from there you'll get your gear and then you'll be taken to Okinawa."

"What happened to Dunbar?"

"He'll be going back to the Rock with you, right now though get some rest, you'll be leaving in the morning."

"I'll try, but with these babies in my arms that won't be easy."

"You'll manage Walters." Stewart smoothly and quickly walked out of the room. I lay there mentally reeling. Omi had turned me in. She must have been forced to do it, there was no way she'd purposely do this; I couldn't accept it. I finally fell into a troubled state of sleeping. Terrified of what could have happened to me.

After being released from sickbay, Dunbar and I were to be quickly sent to Yokota to wait for a flight back to the Rock. Still weak, but eager to travel I quickly packed my gear and left Camp Fuji. The Commanding Officer had to be informed by N.I.S. that I was ordered back to Okinawa. He liked Dunbar and my efforts so much that he didn't want us to leave. He did, however, get upset at me being U.A. for a couple of days. Naval Intelligence didn't want the C.O. to know the story so they concocted a tale for me. Anyway, we left Fuji without me saying goodbye to Gatsuki; I'd miss her.

We were scheduled to leave Mainland as soon as flight was available. Dunbar didn't know the whole story, but he appeared really curious as to my whereabouts the last few days. My weak condition left the Marine thinking I had went on a sex bender. As we waited on the flight, Dunbar, tired of me saying nothing started a conversation: "Hey, Walters, where are you going from the Rock?"

"I'm not sure Dunbar, but believe me, I'm looking forward to it."

"Yeah, I can't wait to get back to the States, man, I really miss American women Walters."

"Are you still going to buy a house Dunbar?"

"Damn right Walters, but I have to finish my enlistment first."

"I kind of figured that Dunbar, but you could purchase it and start making payments on it."

"Thanks, but I'll wait until I'm discharged. By the way where the hell were you Monday, you didn't report to work."

"I was kidnapped Dunbar."

"Right, by some whore, Walters?"

"You're exactly right Dunbar."

"I thought so, you're lucky you didn't get busted Walters, and why did this Marine, Stewart, have to speak up for you?"

"Like I said, I was Kidnapped Dunbar." Dunbar shrugged me off and lay on his rack; I did the same and fell asleep, thankful to be away from the Crazed Fuji.

On the flight back we traveled on a C-130. A rough bumpy ride, we rode for hours. Finally, the thing stumbled down in Okinawa. We disembarked and walked into Kadena. A one hundred pound Gorilla seemed to jump off my back. Our orders had been for us to report to Camp Foster's reception center. A military vehicle waited for us and we boarded and headed to Camp Foster. We would live here for a week and then we'd fly to America. I had to call Yuriko by phone and tell her to be ready to go with me to America in one week. I had to explain to her that yes, it was on short notice, but that I had special orders and there was nothing I could do about it. Yuriko, a willing a faithful wife, was eager to go. I wanted to go over personally and tell her, but I was ordered to stay aboard Base. Before the phone call ended Mary got on the phone and I gave her directions on how to get to Camp Foster.

Thirty minutes later, they had a cab drop them off at the reception center. Yuriko, as soon as she saw me, rushed into my arms. Even Kim gave me a hug. Mary spoke first: "Walters, you go home soon why?"

"It's a long story Mary and I'm not in the mood for telling it." Mary understood and then stated: "We go to America too Walters?"

"Are you sure Mary?" I said with Yuriko still hanging on me. Curious Marines gave me stares as they went to and fro. "Yes, Walters, we are sure. We get ready to leave when you go to States. I let my sister keep my home for me."

"It's very expensive to fly from here Mary."

"I know, we meet you at Los Angeles Airport, we fly the same time you leave Okinawa."

"Okay Mary, that will be fine, I'm looking forward to leaving this place."

"You in some kind of trouble Walters, we have lotta police coming to our home."

"Yes, Mary, I'm into something, but it should be over soon."

"Okay, I believe you. What can we do here on Base, I want to see it."

"Let's catch a movie." I said; we all agreed and headed out to catch a cab to get to the Base Theater.

The week quickly passed. I had received Orders to go to Camp Pendleton, 1st Tank Battalion, but I had 30 days leave in Nebraska first. I had all my gear and I met Yuriko at Kadena. Being married, Yuriko was eligible to fly with me. As she stated, Mary and Kim caught the Japanese Airline. As we boarded the flight, Yuriko seemed frightened: "Walters, I'm not so sure about this, I've never flew on an airplane before."

"Don't worry Yuriko, just sit back and relax."

"I will try Walters." Yuriko said nervously; we had waited in the terminal for an hour before boarding the flight. I chuckled as Yuriko clung tightly to me. We took our seats and strapped in. I watched in amusement at Yuriko as we prepared to leave. She tried to look self-assured, but it didn't work, the nervousness came through like the rays of the Sun: "Relax Yuriko, it will be okay."

"I'm trying Walters, but I can't." Just as Yuriko said that, the Flying Tiger took off. The speed of the take off caught Yuriko off guard, she screamed and tried to fight the energy. "No Yuriko flow with it, you'll be alright." Yuriko remained silent but her eyes were big. The beast finally went airborne. Yuriko appeared to relax somewhat: "I think I will be okay now Walters."

"Good, now try and close your eyes, it's going to be a long flight."

"Do you think Momma son and Kim are okay?"

"Yes, I think they will be fine don't worry Yuriko." She leaned back in her seat, which gave me a clue to relax myself.

When we hit ground again Yuriko was sound asleep. Abruptly awakened by the landing jolt, Yuriko popped up in her seat. "Are we there yet Walters?"

"No, we're in Alaska Yuriko."

"What are we doing in Alaska Walters?"

"I'm not sure Yuriko, we'll see." We then were asked to disembark. We slowly left the huge bird. Yuriko hung on to me closely. She for all her ways was no more than a country girl at best. As we walked in the Alaska terminal, we caught sight of the huge Polar Bear in the middle of the terminal. Yuriko gasped at the spectacle: "Walters, is that real?"

"Yes Yuriko, it's a stuffed Bear, but yes it's real." Yuriko stared in amazement I practically had to pry her eyes off the image and we then walked around the terminal exploring it. Yuriko, excited to travel outside of her world took everything with relish. Finally, we sat down and relaxed. Shortly we were called back on the flight and we headed for America.

When we finally made it to LAX, Mary and Kim waited for us. "What took you so long Walters?"

"We stopped in a couple of places Mary."

"What do we do now?"

"Yuriko and I are going to Nebraska to my grandmother's home, you are welcome of course."

"Yes, we will come with you Walters."

"Okay, Mary, lets book a flight, the sooner the better." We went and booked a flight. I was thankful for Jonah for giving me the money. Then I remembered the Datsun. I'd have to write him and thank him and let him keep the car; He deserved it. I hoped he and Monique well.

After haggling and waiting in the terminal a few hours, we boarded our flight to Nebraska. I hoped my grandmother was prepared for what was coming. I took her to be a religious woman who had tolerance for all people. I worried little about acceptance. By the time we got into Omaha, we had spent over 24 hours flying. Everyone was ready for some sleep. I arranged so that we could get a flight to Lincoln and then we could possibly get someone to help us with our luggage. When we finally got to Lincoln, I was so exhausted I wanted to sleep right at the terminal, but

I knew I couldn't; I telephoned my grandmother: "Hello grandmother, this is Everett." I had been going by Walters for so long, I had almost said it to grandmother. "Everett, well, I'll be son, it's been almost one year, and how have you been?"

"Great, grandmother, I'm at the Airport here in Lincoln, so I'll be home shortly and I have a surprise for you Grandmother."

"I wonder what on earth it is Everett?"

"You'll see; and grandmother is there anyway I can get a hold of dad?" Grandmother hesitated before replying: "Yes, he's here Everett, he's here. He will be so happy to see you Everett and so will I."

"Love you Grandmother and I'll see you shortly."

"I love you too son and I will leave the door open for you okay."

"Thank you, Grandmother." We said our goodbyes for now and I turned my attention to the girls. "Listen Mary we need to get a cab or two and transport all of our belongings to my grandmother's home." I realized that Mary didn't have a lot of luggage with her, so that might help us. Kim traveled light as well. We called a taxi service and packed our gear into two taxis. I gave both drivers my address and Yuriko and I took one cab and Mary and Kim taking the other.

I was on American soil, back home where it all started, but I was more than the innocent boy that left almost two years ago. I purposely didn't tell grandmother of Yuriko mainly out of fear of what she'd say. Now while I understood my grandmother not to be prejudiced, I learned in the Corps even well-meaning people had viewpoints that startled me.

I had learned from Stewart that the Corps wanted me off the Islands as quickly as possible. I never went in front of a hearing or anything, which I was sure, had to take place. Stewart told me that at my new duty station that I'd get an ear full I expected it. Meanwhile Yuriko and I rode in silence to my home. Yuriko appeared to tremble as I held her loosely. The cabbie noticing my uniform broke the silence. "Where are you coming from Jarhead?"

"Japan sir!"

"Yeah, that's obvious, what part?"

"Mainland Japan and Okinawa." I mentioned ever so politely.

"Well," the driver responded: "I spent a little time in Nam, I came on the last Boat ride."

"Who did you serve with?" I asked, the driver spitting out of the window in the process. The cool morning air hitting me like a wave. "I served in the Navy for 2 years young man until I was discharged for alcohol abuse, but I enjoyed my tour, I've been a cab driver ever since." The driver seemed to relish his occupation so I went ahead and fueled his ego: "I drive vehicles in the Marines you know."

"Oh really, well, how do you like the experience as a driver, Marine?"

"I really enjoyed it to be honest, I saw a lot of things I'd never seen had I not been a driver."

"Listen young man, if you want to drive cabs for a living let me know I'll put in a good word for you."

"Thanks, but I'll be okay sir." I couldn't believe the unassuming fellow actually thought I'd like this kind of work. Sure, it was money but…the conversation went quiet; the driver begins humming as he drove on. A half an hour later we came upon familiar turf. I began scouring the neighborhood for people hanging around. Everyone must have been at work or school because things were barren. The cabbie pulled into our driveway: "Here you are young man and remember what I said."

"I will." I paid the steep fare and thanked the driver. As we took out our belongings I could see the driver suspiciously eyeing Yuriko, but not saying anything. He looked as though liquor had robbed him of his health. His eyes were blood shot and his appearance haggard. He had perhaps a few years at best before he fell apart. After getting the luggage I let the driver keep the change. We waited a few minutes for Mary and Kim, when they arrived, we walked to the front door. "So this is where you live Walter, it's very nice." Mary said impressed. I had to admit this was not the worst neighborhood. Grandmother really took care of things.

I rang the doorbell twice before a tired looking grandmother opened the door. "Everett!" Grandmother screamed. I rushed to hug her; grandmother embraced me tightly before she noticed the others. "And who are these lovely people?"

"Grandmother, this is my wife Yuriko and her mother Mary and her sister Kim."

"Well, hello, all of you." Grandmother gave each girl a hug. "Why don't all of you come in and put your bags away."

"Grandmother did you tell dad?" Grandmother looked sadly at me and turned away.

"What's wrong Grandmother is dad okay?" Grandmother took me be the hand.

"Sweetheart I don't know how to tell you this, but your father lost his sanity several months ago. The doctors say it's an early form of dementia; rare but reality." Grandmother hugged me tight again. "Oh Everett, your father was doing so well, he even had begun a political career, it happened so suddenly."

"Why didn't anyone tell me!" I screamed anger suddenly filling my body. "You had enough troubles, Everett. We heard about the things you were going through. Your friend Madison Bilkens told us and don't worry Everett, your father doesn't know."

"Where's mom Grandmother?"

"I don't know Everett, she left him soon after his illness struck." Stunned, I couldn't do anything but cry. I shuddered and screamed like I had stepped on hot fire. Yuriko tried to comfort me and Mary also, but the emptiness of my family being torn shattered me. I didn't know what to do. I calmed a bit and shaking from grief I asked Grandmother: "Where is he Grandmother?"

"He's in your old room Everett, he has a Nurse who keeps him sedated most of the time. If you can help it, please don't let him see your wife Everett he'll explode."

"Grandmother, are you telling me dad's prejudiced!"

"Very, Everett; ever since Vietnam he's held animosity toward Orientals." I soaked in everything I heard. Mary heard and stiffened. My father did experience hard realities in the war and I had to respect his viewpoint, but this was my family now and I loved them too. "Can I see him Grandmother?"

"Yes, child, go to him." I nervously walked in the room to see the man whom I had grown to love as my dad. He sat in a chair near the bed. "Everett!"

Whisper Alley

"Yes Dad?"

"Come here son." I quickly went to my father:

"Here I am Dad."

"Maybe you'll listen to me son. I've talked with God and he said I wasn't crazy."

"No, Dad, you're not, you're my father."

"I know son, and I am telling the angels to get me out of this place, I need to talk to the President right away. Drive me there, son." Dad went to stand up. Still a formidable man at six three, I tried to reason with my father. "Look, Dad, I'll call the White House and send word that you need the President, get some rest now." Just then Mary and the girls peeked in, dad saw them and scrambled to get under the bed: "Commies, Commies, get cover!"

"No dad this is my wife, not Commies, they're friends."

"No gook's a friend of mine." Dad came out from under the bed with a stick. I had to grab it. "Careful dad you don't want to hurt anyone, calm down dad, we all love you here." Mary seemed to make sense of it all. She walked over to dad and begin to stroke his arm. "It will be okay Mr. Walters, it will be okay." This seemed to reassure my who settled down somewhat. Yuriko and Kim walked closer to dad; he started relaxing.

"Good, now I'm Mary and these two girls belong to me." My dad responded by smiling at Mary. Grandmother, who was crying perked up a bit. "Well, I'll be, he's really liking the attention. Mary again spoke up: "Well, you have to be gentle he is okay." I relaxed a little, but being shook up over dad's condition I couldn't understand this happening so quickly. As soon as we got dad back in his bed, his Nurse came into the room. "How's my Tiger today?" Dad responded well to his Nurse. After we all introduced ourselves, I left the room. Grandmother came after me. "Everett, I have something else to tell you."

"What's that Grandmother?"

"Madison has a young child that she say's is yours." The cement truck hit me hard. A child, boy it really came at me in waves now. "How does she know it's mine Grandmother?"

171

"She's positive it's yours son and she seems to think you're going to be with her." Before I knew it, Mary came out of the room. "Is this true Walters, you have a son without our knowledge?"

"I'm not sure Mary, this is all news to me."

"When did you meet her?" Mary asked quite angrily.

"Overseas, right when I met Yuriko." If looks could kill, I'd be a dead man. Mary's look said it all. She trusted me with her daughter's life and virginity, and I did this in return to her daughter. "Look, I'm sorry Mary, but I didn't know it would come out like this. Mary held her tongue out of respect for my Grandmother. I observed in horror as Mary went and broke the news to Yuriko, who broke down in tears. Torn, I stood there helpless to do anything. As I caught Grandmother's attention, she had an ever so slight twinkle in her smile.

CHAPTER SIXTEEN
MY WAY

As I expected, Mary and the girls slept in the spare room at my grandmother's home. They also refused dinner choosing to stay in the room the whole evening. What ripped my heart out, the next morning, Mary and the girls said, "goodbye." I vehemently tried protesting: "Mary, I'm married to your daughter, you can't leave!"

"Walter, you not honest with me. You say you love Yuriko, not go and have child with another woman!"

"I'm sorry Mary, but I made a mistake."

"I know Walters, and I'm not mad at you, but I can't trust you." Yuriko came over and gave me the checkbook and her military I.D. card: "I won't be needing these, Walters."

"But where are you going Mary?"

"We have family here in America, I told you before, I'm used to this country."

"Please Mary…" I didn't know what else to say. This is not how I expected my vacation to turn out. Too many things were happening to me. I wasn't sure if I could pull through this, but I had too. I still had over one year of duty to the Corps and I'd fulfill that regardless of the circumstances. Mary and the girls came and hugged me. "Goodbye Walters." I walked outside with them as they got into the taxi. After they left, I slowly went back into the house. Grandmother was there waiting. "Everett, what on earth were you thinking overseas."

"What do you mean Grandmother?"

"Now, I understand you sleeping with whores, but marriage, son, you have a lot to learn about life."

"But Grandmother."

"No Everett, listen, you have worked too hard to lose your earnings and life to a bunch of second-class citizens."

"You really mean that Grandmother?"

"Son, Madison is a nice girl, settle down with her."

"She's the whore Grandmother!" The force of the slap startled me.

"I don't ever want to hear of you speaking like that of her Everett, as a matter of fact she's coming over for dinner tonight and she's bringing the baby. So get used to it!"

"I knew it was hard marrying interracially, but I never knew Grandmother to be so rigid. Yuriko leaving tore my heart out. I had planned to love her for the remainder of my life. Mary surprised me. After I learned of dad's illness, I thought she'd have a heart, but now I didn't have Yuriko at all in my life.

As planned, Madison came over for dinner and she brought the baby. I had to admit I was pleasantly surprised; a jolly bundle of joy and to top it off the baby was a boy. All the pain and heartache melted away as I viewed the young life. I observed Madison, she had been quiet all evening. Looking hard at me she finally spoke: "So where's your wife Everett?"

"They heard the news of you and I and strangely enough they left this morning."

"You mean they left for Japan?"

"I have no idea Madison, but why did you come to my grandmother with this."

"It's the only way to get your attention Everett, besides I'm keeping in touch with Natalie and she's told me plenty. I knew you really didn't like the Okinawan whore."

"Is that what you told my grandmother?"

"She asked, so I explained to her your little indiscretions Everett."

"What about you and Thorn, Madison?"

"Just a tool, I knew he had a beef with you so I wanted to see your metal."

"Did you like it, Madison?"

"Yes I did, I had no idea you'd kick him like that!"

"I had no choice, Madison." Madison smiled and licked her chops. "Anyway Everett, I'll wait until your divorce is final, she may come back and I don't want anything to do with those dangerous slanted eyed winches."

"Well if she does Madison, I'll be sure and tell you." I let the sarcasm run openly. Grandmother, who had checked on dad came back in the room: "How's everything you two?"

"Fine Grandmother, we're reliving old times that's all."

"Well, that's good Everett, maybe you'll see what it's like to be with a real woman for a change."

"What's that supposed to mean Grandmother?"

"Son, being with whores for so long and then bringing them to my doorstep is just too much Everett, I did this for your own good."

"Well Grandmother in the future, I'd like to make my own decisions."

"Sure Everett, as soon as you grow up." Grandmother winked at Madison before leaving the dining room. Madison smiled and continued: "I still can't believe your wife left so soon."

"It was her mother's idea Madison."

"You brought her mother too Everett!"

"Yes, we planned on sharing an apartment together at my duty station in California, but we never sat down and made plans. I should have never come here."

"Cheer up Everett, you know how difficult it would have been with an interracial marriage nowadays."

"I could have made it work Madison. Times have changed you know."

"Not here in Lincoln they haven't, it's still the same way it's always been."

"I don't think so Madison." We went back and forth for a few minutes getting to know each other again.

I had stayed at home for the majority of my leave. I didn't feel comfortable going too far away from home. I wanted to stay as close as possible to dad as I could. He was in and out of reality. I understood why the Army discharged him, he had become a danger to any military units integrity. I took dad's illness hard; how could this all be happening to me. It seemed as though the higher powers had it in for me and there was no way to avoid the calamities that befell me. I went out with Madison and the baby once, we went out and had some ice cream at the local store. Lincoln hadn't changed much, but I had; I really held a grudge against Madison for everything, she knew herself to be a manipulating woman who wanted to control no matter who she hurt. Grandmother was just a pawn in Madison scheme. Both grandmother and I grew apart on my leave. I think grandmother meant well and she wanted to keep the family together, but I knew in my heart that Yuriko meant more to me than the love of dad and grandmother. I kept the peace at home not wanting to hurt grandmother any further. Dad had hurt her enough; his illness had torn the family in two.

When my month passed, I prepared to leave. Mary had called and left me an address to reach her in California. Gratefully grandmother didn't know. She had left for church early that morning. Grandmother had said her goodbyes to me thinking that Madison and I would be a family. I liked Madison, but I couldn't trust her now. The baby could well be Thorn's, who knows. My main concern was at least being on speaking terms with Yuriko. I didn't want to see my dad today, so I left him with his Nurse. The more time I spent around him the more I saw the disorder. He couldn't stay focused on one thing and he had lost track that he once held the honor of being an Officer in the United States Army. There was even talk of it being mad cow disease, but we couldn't be sure. The Nurse had limited knowledge of the matter and she did her best to make dad as comfortable as possible. She even got in his bed when grandmother wasn't around. Through it all dad still had desires for females; mom really surprised me leaving the way she did, her man still needed her. As the cab came, I packed my gear in it and headed out.

When I arrived at 1st Tank Battalion some two days later, a team of Naval Intelligence men welcomed me. The one who introduced himself first was Lieutenant Jerome Roberson, a black youthful looking man no more than 25: "Hello, Lance corporal Walters. At ease Marine, we want to welcome you back to the States, how was your leave?"

"Fine sir."

"Did you see your father son?"

"Yes sir, I did."

"We are terribly sorry about your family crises son, it's a damn shame, your dad a good man. Walters the reason why we're here is son we liked the way you handled yourself on Okinawa, I mean you could have went to pieces and to go through what you must have went through on leave, well…" The Lieutenant went silent. The other two men were enlisted and they took notes. Roberson abruptly started talking again. "Lance corporal, we'd like you to join us son. You'd be a valuable asset to the Marine Corps and you'd get some valuable training. Perhaps you could even serve near your home town." I didn't have to think long about the offer, I wanted to give the military back what I took.

"I'd be glad too Lieutenant."

"Good, now if you go through the motions of checking into your unit, afterwards we'll come and get you and we'll inform you on what to do next. That understood Marine!"

"Yes sir, very clear sir!" The lieutenant handed me a form and he and his aides left Headquarters. I went to my unit to check in and ran into the C.O. Captain R. Winters greeted me. "Have a seat Marine."

"Yes sir." I sat on one of the two chairs in the Captain's office. A very colorful decorated place it appeared that Captain Winters had some experience in Infantry. A large man who carried his bulk lithely. Squared jaws with a high and tight, gung-ho all the way. I had better be careful with my C. O. The Captain spoke first: "Listen Marine scuttlebutt says that you lived dangerous on the Rock and not in a manner befitting a U.S. Marine, anything to say for yourself."

"Sir, I didn't understand the ways of the Orient and yes I paid a heavy price for it sir, but I lived in a manner that honored the Corps sir."

"Where did you go to school Walters?"

"I went to Community College in Nebraska sir, one day I'll try for my Bachelor's."

"I see Walters, very impressive. As you know you will be going straight to Naval training, so after you check in young man off you go. After you check in report to me tomorrow at 0700 hours. You won't be used here Walters."

"Yes sir!"

"Dismissed Corporal." I did an about face trying to make certain I heard the Captain say Corporal. Damn! "Ooorrah". I walked away from the Captain's office trying to figure out where I needed to go to check in.

After hours I got Mary's address out and headed outside the Gate. Mary lived near downtown San Diego. It should be easy to find her. It was well after 1600, I stepped on the Greyhound Bus after Base transportation took me outside the Gate. I rode to Downtown San Diego. I took out Mary's information and called the number on it. After a few rings and older voice answered when I said "Is Mary there?"

"Mary?"

"Yes."

"One moment please." I waited patiently until I heard Mary's voice: "Hello, this is Mary."

"Hello Mary this is Walters, I'm in California."

"Where are you now Walters?"

"I'm at the Greyhound Bus station."

"Wait there, we'll come and get you."

"Okay Mary, I'll wait for you." I put down the phone and looked around the station. The dregs and outcast roamed freely throughout the station. I saw Navy and Marine personnel skittering along. I looked off would be peddlers and women plying their trades. 20 minutes or so later I saw Mary walk through the front door. I quickly went to meet her: "Mary!"

"Come on Walters, let's get to my place we need to talk." We quickly went outside and Mary led me to a nice-looking Oldsmobile Cutlass. An older Oriental man sat behind the wheel. Mary led me to the back seat. We seated ourselves and then drove away from the terminal. "Walters, this is my uncle."

"Hello sir." The older man nodded his head, but did not turn around. We drove into downtown and into residential neighborhoods. "We will stay with my uncle until we find a place Walters."

"How's Yuriko Mary?"

"She went back to Okinawa Walters." It hit me like a knife in the back: "Okinawa!"

"Yes, you broke her heart into pieces and she couldn't go on with out you Walters."

"Mary I'm sorry my grandmother set me up, she didn't like Oriental people." I couldn't help but cry, Yuriko, the love I never really loved was now gone. "Is she coming back Mary?"

"I don't know Walter, Kim is in school, she likes San Diego."

"What will Yuriko do in Okinawa Mary?"

"She will live at my place with my sister. She will be fine Walter, maybe you see her again." The gentleman drove into an apartment complex. We all got out and went into the apartment.

The air had been taken out of my lungs; I really didn't know why Mary wanted me over now that Yuriko was not there. Once inside the apartment, Mary Uncle left the living room. "Sit down Walters." I took a seat. "You know I understand how your family feels, we are strange people to them. Everything happened so fast. So, they don't like us." Mary grimly added a little disturbed.

"The important thing is I like you Mary that's what counts."

"I believe you Walters, and I should have stopped Yuriko, but she very sad." I remained silent and watched as Mary left the room. Seconds later Kim came out. Shy and soft-spoken she came out and sat down. "Hello Kim."

"Hi." She said with her head down and before I knew it Mary stuck her head out of the door and said "anything Walters." I took clue.

As time went on, I received orders from Naval Investigation to work right here aboard Camp Pendleton. It turned out that the Navy wanted me to work in the field spying on would be drug dealers on Base. They used me as Drug Dealer who made contacts with unscrupulous dealers, which I kept, note on and kept Intelligence posted. Not a bad job, but the training for 6 months was brutal. I had learned valuable techniques about drugs and fraudulent behavior. After I informed Intelligence about the drug dealers they were busted, and no one would know I was involved. Okinawa taught me well. I received my discharge over a year later. Navy Brass wanted me to stay, but I had bigger fish to fry. They even offered me $15000. A lot of money, but I had something lined up in San Diego. As I was sent to reception for discharge Navy Brass informed me that Filson received 10 years at Leavenworth. He had committed an armed robbery before his discharge; what a stupid man. He was scot-free, I didn't pity him.

As much as I loved grandma and Madison and dad, I wasn't ready to go back to Lincoln. I decided to love my memory of them. However, I did have a neighbor inform me of their whereabouts. For now, I loved Kim. Mary knew that I was a good provider and Kim met my needs for right now. I never loved her the way I did Yuriko, but she had beautiful ways, so I stayed with her. I still let Mary and her uncle, who turned out to be her lover, live with me. I had purchased a home in Lajolla.

I found a job working for a law firm in Lajolla investigating fraudulent injury cases. Military training was paramount to me getting the job. I had been on the job 6 months after my discharge. The money was excellent and I used it to the full. I remember taking Mary and Kim shopping one day and buying them both new wardrobes. Both girls had grown on me, but I still missed Yuriko. Late one August, I had a vacation due, which of course I'd travel to Okinawa alone. I had made an excuse telling Mary and Kim that I needed to see Grandmother. Preparing for the trip I had to be careful. I had all of Yuriko's paperwork just incase I found her. I travel light; I'd just have to wash often. I also brought along Yuriko's favorite summer dress.

I boarded a military flight at LAX to Okinawa. Everyone one else was in uniform, so I looked out of place, sort of like a rich kid. It felt good for a change to gloat. After a long and challenging flight, we touched down in Okinawa. I couldn't believe I was here again after all I had been through; still I had to press on. When I got all of my gear, I went to BEQ and rented a room. This was safer and cheaper and Yuriko would be safe once she got to this point. After freeing myself of everything I checked the time. 10:00 Monday night. The jet lag would hit me soon, that's a long trip, I spent over twelve hours on the air liner, still wobbly I headed for Gate Two. From there I caught a cab over to Mary's old place no one lived there. Disappointed I decided to hang out on Gate Two Street. Jonah had reenlisted in the Corps and still was stationed on the Rock. I'd stop by and see Jonah, Monique and the baby. Jonah would be glad to see me after all this time. I was amused at how time flew. I had went to Lidos and looked in. Same racket different people; I decided to have a drink and relax for a while. Thinking of all my exploits here on the Island startled me. I couldn't believe I had done the things I did. The women, the drugs, the fast car; I had become an animal and didn't know it. The Corps built character and I used it for my own ends. Certain I wasn't career material I still felt grateful for my time in the World's Finest. I chuckled at the antics the Drill Instructors used to motivate new recruits; it stuck with me throughout the years.

For old times sake I left Lidos and decided to walk down Whisper Alley. It held the same decrepit buildings, and the smell of sulfur permeated the air. Even the containers of salt were in place. I saw the women at work. As I took a slow tour down the Alley, I swore I heard someone calling my name. I followed the sound of the voice. As I got closer and saw whom it was, it hit me like a freightliner, Yuriko! I couldn't describe how I felt; hurt, anger, sadness. All those emotions wanted to scream out, but my wisdom of the Alley taught me that screaming spelled trouble. I calmly walked toward Yuriko. She put her finger over her mouth, so I remained silent. "Walters." She whispered, "You came back!" I nodded my head trying to stop the tears from flowing, but they fell anyway. Yuriko took me by the hand and led me into a back room. Zombie like I followed her.

We got into her cubicle. Yuriko motioned for me to sit down. I sat and she began whispering in my ear: "Walters, they are forcing me to do this, my aunt died and I couldn't pay for anything and I…" Yuriko stopped in mid sentence;

"It's okay Yuriko, I'll get you out of here."

"How Walters?" I knew Yuriko got time off from work.

"Where do you go when you're not here Yuriko?"

"I live here, I sleep when I'm not working, I hate it." Yuriko buried her face in my lap. I had to stay strong for her. "Listen Yuriko, meet me by the Air Force Base on Gate Two tomorrow at noon, can you do that?"

"Yes, Walters, no one will be watching in the daytime." I knew that I had to sleep with Yuriko, so no one would get suspicious. "Undress Yuriko."

"Okay, you're right Walters." Yuriko undressed quickly. I could see she had gotten used to this, but I still loved her. I undressed and we went through the motion of cheap sex. Yuriko tried to be passionate, but I knew it wasn't in her heart. I went at it for a few minutes and rolled off of her. "You okay Walters?"

"No Yuriko, I'm not, but don't worry, I'll get you out of here!"

"I know you will Walters." I turned away from Yuriko and got dressed. She watched as I walked out of the room. I had put a $20 bill on the table, thinking of Yuriko's boss and the beating she might get if she didn't collect the money.

I walked trance like toward the Air Base. There was a payphone that I could use to call Jonah. When I called the phone rang three times before a tired sounding Jonah answered: "Hello, Jonah speaking."

"Hello Jonah, this is Everett Walters, how are you?"

"I've been better friend, what's up with this call so late, I'm in bed."

"Listen Jonah, I need a favor."

"Yes?"

"I'm at Gate Two Street near the Entrance of Kadena, I need a place to stay for a few hours."

"Sure Everett, but you will need to get a ride here, I can't leave right now."

"Okay give me the address and I'll catch a cab." Jonah carefully gave me the address and I remembered it. I hailed one of the few cabs in the area and gave him directions, I'd see my friend after over a year of running seemingly everywhere.

When the cab driver dropped me off at Base Housing in front of Jonah's unit, Jonah stood there with the door open. I paid the cab driver and quickly got out of the car. "Hello Walters, long time no see." Jonah had gained some weight since I last seen him.

"Same here Jonah." As I walked to the door Jonah, expecting to see me in uniform commented on it: "where's your uniform and luggage Walters?"

"I'm discharged Walters, and I rented a room on Kadena."

"So you're a civilian now, huh, Walters?"

"Yeah, I work for a law firm in Lajolla California."

"You sly dog you, how did you manage that?"

"The Marine Corps has been good to me Jonah, I really can't explain it, but I've benefited greatly from my enlistment."

"So what brings you to Okinawa?"

"My wife Jonah, I came for my wife."

"Where is she?" I looked at Jonah and almost broke down.

"She's on Whisper Alley." Jonah's mouth dropped. Being the suave New Yorker, he didn't comment, yet I knew he had a thousand questions. "I know Jonah, it's an unusual story to say the least, but I'm still in love with her and we are going to escape from this Island tomorrow."

"How Everett?"

"I'm technically still married to her and I do have current I. D. status on her. That will make getting her out of here so easy, all I have to do is get her to Kadena before the mob catches on. If we get out before working hours, we'll have a head start. So as soon as we can we are flying out of here Jonah." Jonah understood me completely nodding his head; just then Monique came out of the room in a see-through nightgown acting as if I weren't there. Jonah said nothing. I avoided eye contact with Monique, but I got an eye full of the ample but sharply feline. Jonah ignored his wife's appearance. "Oh, hi, Walters, long time no see, you'll have to get a peek at our son when you get a chance."

"Yes, I'll do that Monique, that will be nice."

"Excuse me, but I fell a draft." Jonah burst into laughter. I felt bad enough about Yuriko, so I remained silent. Monique slipped back into the bedroom. "She doesn't get much company so she wants to show off."

"I see, and you're alright with that Jonah?"

"Hey, it's her home too you know."

"That's true Jonah." Hoping to get back on the subject of Yuriko I added. "You know Jonah, she left the States angry at me, I only wish she could have been more patient."

"Why's she leave the States Walters?"

"My family was against interracial marriage and they pried her loose from me. You remember Madison, Jonah?"

"Yes, how can I forget the tall shapely bombshell."

"Well, she filled my grandmother's head up with lies and they hurt Yuriko with them, so she decided to leave me." Jonah whistled:

"That doesn't sound like a good idea on her part, she must have been awfully upset." Jonah, still in his skivvies, realized the time. "Listen Walters, crash on the couch, I have to get to work in the morning."

"Sure, Jonah, by the way, what's your rank now?"

"You're looking at a proud Sergeant, Walters!"

"That's great Marine, glad to hear it."

"Simper Fi Walters, I'm hitting the rack."

"Pleasant dreams Jonah."

"Yes, I plan on it." I chuckled at the wisdom of my comrade. I took off my loafers and lay on the couch. Thinking of the love for Yuriko I fell into a listless sleep.

As she stated Monique had her baby groomed and ready for inspection. I gave the young child rave reviews. Monique thanked me and quickly left. She had to get the baby to a sitter and she had to get to her job of teaching high school. Jonah, the slick bastard, had really put his hooks in Monique; she really appeared to love him. I gave Monique a hug and wished her well. Then I waited for Jonah: "Hey listen, Walters, I really liked the car you left, but a Squid wanted it and he gave me $5000 for it."

"Really? I guess I only owe you $15000 now."

"Well just stay ready Monique and I are going to have to come visit you in California."

"Here, I'll give you my address." I threw some water on my face and Jonah took me over to Kadena. I thanked my bosom buddy and wished him well. I couldn't get over Jonah's integrity. A real tough and ready man he took what he wanted in life. I looked at the time. Maybe 15 minutes before 8:00 a.m. I decided to eat chow and then check the manifest and see when I could get Yuriko out of here. After eating I made the long walk to the terminal to kill time. When I got there I'd have to wait several days before flying to LAX. A bit perturbed, but at least we'd be out of Okinawa.

When 12:00 noon rolled around I waited for Yuriko. She showed up like clockwork. She had dressed casual which was good. No need to bring undue attention to herself. I ushered her through the gates, the Guards giving us little trouble. I looked around to see if anyone followed us. Yuriko had done well; no one appeared to catch on. I took Yuriko to my room aboard Kadena. When I shut the door Yuriko came over to me and fell into my arms. "I'm so glad it's over Walters, if you didn't love me enough to come back, I'd have become a useless old woman."

"Don't think about that Yuriko, just be glad that I found you in time." Yuriko clung tightly to me trying to gather herself. She had been through a nightmare and now she had escaped with my help. I was so fortunate that I knew exactly what to do and avoid a confrontation with the underworld figures involved in prostituting women. With all the sadness in my life, it was about time I got a chance to win. I really liked Kim and now I found Yuriko. Madison, young woman who knew what strings to pull on anyone she could put her clutches on didn't destroy me like she wanted. I took Yuriko back after all. I gave Yuriko a tight hug and kissed her forehead; and I realized that I had grown into a man on my terms.

Yuriko and I had to settle for a flight to Korea. From there we'd have to wait for a flight to the States when our names would come up on the manifest. When we took our seats, I heard a woman talking to a man seated next to her. I stood up trying to connect the voice with a body. As I zeroed in on the voice it hit me; Omi! I quickly sat down, what the hell that meant only time had the answer.

www.ingramcontent.com/pod-product-compliance
Ingram Content Group UK Ltd.
Pitfield, Milton Keynes, MK11 3LW, UK
UKHW041944131224
452403UK00004B/398